He's impatient...

He's impossible...

But he's absolutely irresistible!

He's...

Her Italian Boss

Two original stories to celebrate
Valentine's Day by your favorite
Presents authors, together in one volume!

LYNNE GRAHAM was born in Northern Ireland and has been a keen Harlequin reader since her teens. She is very happily married with an understanding husband, who has learned to cook since she started to write! Her five children keep her on her toes. She has two dogs—one large who knocks everything over and a tiny terrier who has a big bark. When time allows, Lynne is a keen gardener.

KIM LAWRENCE lives on a farm in rural Wales. She runs two miles daily and finds this an excellent opportunity to unwind and seek inspiration for her writing. It also helps her keep up with her husband, two active sons and the various stray animals that have adopted them. Always a fanatical reader of books, she is now equally enthusiastic about writing. She loves a happy ending!

Lynne Graham
Kim Lawrence

HER ITALIAN BOSS

TORONTO • NEW YORK • LONDON
AMSTERDAM • PARIS • SYDNEY • HAMBURG
STOCKHOLM • ATHENS • TOKYO • MILAN • MADRID
PRAGUE • WARSAW • BUDAPEST • AUCKLAND

ISBN 0-373-12302-7

HER ITALIAN BOSS

First North American Publication 2003.

Copyright © 2003 by Lynne Graham and Kim Lawrence.

Lynne Graham

THE BOSS'S VALENTINE

CHAPTER ONE

IT HAD been a hideous day at work.

On the way home, Poppy called into the corner shop and the first thing she noticed was that the big valentine card she had admired over a month earlier was still unsold. She couldn't understand why nobody had bought it for she loved its glorious overblown pink roses and simple sentimental verse. She wondered why all the cards her more fortunate friends received were joke ones with comic, cruel, or even crude messages.

On an impulse, Poppy lifted the card and decided to buy it. Why shouldn't she send a valentine card? True, nobody had ever sent *her* one, but that didn't mean that she couldn't use the card as a means of brightening someone else's day. As to the identity of that special, lucky someone, there was no doubt in her mind about who would receive the card...

Poppy had fallen head over heels in love with Santino Aragone in her first week working at Aragone Systems. She was all too well aware that Santino was as out of her reach as the moon. Santino was a hugely successful entrepreneur, blessed by spectacular sleek, dark Italian looks, and he had a never-ending string of gorgeous women in his life. But in an emergency Santino Aragone could also be incredibly kind. On her first day at work, when she'd got her finger trapped in a door, Santino had taken her to the hospital himself. When he had fainted dead away at the sight of a needle, Poppy had known he was the man for her...she had thought that was so sweet.

Starry-eyed over the idea that her small, anonymous gesture of a card might at least bring a brief smile to Santino Aragone's brooding dark features on what she knew would be a difficult day for him, she was unlocking the door of her bedsit before her thoughts roamed uneasily back to her own horrendous day at work.

Desmond, the slick new head of marketing, had asked her if

she had been born stupid or perhaps she'd got that way with effort? Having spilt coffee on his keyboard, Poppy had cleaned it up without telling him and in the process somehow wiped his morning's work from his computer. Although she had made grovelling apologies, Desmond had still put in a complaint about her to Human Resources and she had been issued with a formal warning.

Her colleagues would have been surprised to learn that Poppy, famed for her laid-back nature, was even angrier with herself than Desmond had been. If she had not been so busy chatting, the coffee would never have been spilt. Time and time again, a lapse in concentration led to similar mistakes on her part. Sometimes she wondered if the problem had started when she was at school and her parents had, without ever meaning to, managed to undermine her every small triumph.

'I'm sure you've done your best,' her mother would say with a slight grimace when she scanned Poppy's school reports. 'We can't expect you to match Peter's results, can we?'

Her elder brother, Peter, had been born gifted and his achievements had set an impossible standard against which her more average abilities sank without trace. Punch-drunk with pride over their son's academic successes, her parents had always concentrated their energies on Peter. Poppy would have liked to go to university, too, but when she was fifteen, her parents had told her that, as further education was so expensive and Peter would still be completing his doctorate, she would have to leave school and train for a job instead. It had seemed to her then that there was no point in striving for better grades. But it had been a conviction that she had since lived to regret.

Now painfully conscious that she didn't have much in the way of academic qualifications and that she had been lucky to get a position in a slick city business, Poppy worked hard as a marketing assistant. She was willing, enthusiastic and popular with her colleagues, but employees who made foolish mistakes were frowned on at Aragone Systems. In addition, the warning she had received that day was her second in six months and if there was a third, she could be sacked. Ironically, it was not so much the fear of being fired that sent a chill down her taut spine,

it was the terrifying knowledge that if she was fired she would
never, ever set eyes on Santino Aragone again…

'Is this someone's idea of a joke?' Santino Aragone demanded
with incredulous bite when he opened the giant envelope two
days later and found himself looking at the most naff of valentine cards awash with chintzy roses in improbable clashing
pinks.

'I'm as surprised as you are.' His PA, Craig Belston, thought
with considerable amusement that no woman could have chosen
a worse way of trying to impress his sophisticated employer. Or
indeed a worse day or even year to make such a declaration.

The staff Christmas party had been postponed after the sudden
death of Santino's father, Maximo, and rescheduled to take place
as a Valentine's Day event this evening. As bad luck would have
it, Santino was attending another funeral of an old schoolfriend
that very afternoon. Furthermore, it might be a little-known fact
but Santino loathed Valentine's Day in much the same way that
Scrooge had loathed the festive season.

Lean, strong face grim, Santino opened the card. A faint whiff
of an eerily familiar perfume made his nostrils flare and he
frowned. Floral…jasmine? An old-fashioned scent, not the type
of fragrance worn by a stylish woman. But so taken aback was
he by the candid message on the inside of the card that he forgot
about the perfume.

'As always, I'm thinking of you and loving you today,' ran
the screed.

Had he become the unwitting target of some dreadful schoolgirl with a crush? Wincing at the very idea while he mentally
ran through the very few teenage girls within his social circle,
he made no demur when Craig took the liberty of turning the
card round to peruse it for himself.

'Tinkerbell…' Craig pronounced in a tone of raw disbelief.

'I beg your pardon?' Santino prompted drily.

'That dippy redhead in marketing. We call her Tinkerbell because she's always flying about and putting her feet in it noisily.
Well, Poppy's certainly stuck her silly head above the parapet
this time,' the younger man remarked with an unpleasant smile.

'I'm certain she sent this card. That's her scent. She always wears it and guess who loves pink and flowers as well?'

Poppy Bishop, the marketing junior, hired six months ago by his late father in total defiance of HR's choice of candidate while Santino had been on vacation. Why? Maximo had felt sorry for her because she had confided that it was her first interview after fifty-odd job applications. Poppy with her shy but sunny smiles, explosive Titian corkscrew curls and her comical penchant for floral prints and insane diets. Even in a large staff, Poppy was hard to ignore and calamity did follow her around.

'Some women just *live* to embarrass themselves,' Craig remarked thinly. 'Shouldn't someone have a word with her about this? The cheek of her too…a little nobody like her making up to the boss!'

Summoning up a recollection of how Poppy behaved in his vicinity, Santino decided she very probably *was* the culprit. He knew he made her nervous. Around him, she was more than usually clumsy, tongue-tied to the point of idiocy and enveloped in a continual hot blush. She also had a way of looking at him that suggested that with very little effort he might walk on water. Other women treated him to the same look but where they were concerned it was deliberate flattery, whereas Poppy's expressive face paraded her every thought like a banner. He was relieved that she had not signed the card. She would not have appreciated that her trade-mark perfume and love of flowers might be a giveaway and would undoubtedly cringe if she realised that she was even under suspicion. Instantly, Santino regretted allowing Craig to read the card.

'I doubt that Poppy Bishop sent it,' Santino murmured in a bored tone of dismissal as he dropped the card straight into the bin. 'She's just not the type. I imagine it's more likely to have come from some schoolgirl, possibly the daughter of one of my friends. Now, since we've had our entertainment for the day, could you get me the MD of Delsen Industries on the phone?'

Later that morning, Santino's attention wandered back to the bin where the card lay forlorn and rejected. A groan of exasperation escaped his wide, sensual mouth. What on earth had possessed her? His PA hated her guts and would do her a bad turn if he got the chance. Why? Craig was famous for hitting on the youngest, newest female employees, treating them to a one-night stand and then dumping them.

But when his PA had tried his routine on Poppy, she had turned him down and admitted that she had been told that he was the office romeo on her first day, a put-down that had hit Craig's ego right where it hurt. Craig would have been more humiliated, however, had he realised that Santino had been the one to issue that warning. He still didn't know why he had bothered. Maybe it was the fact that his father had warmed to the girl; maybe it was the sheer naivety he had seen in her blue pansy-coloured eyes...

Around ten o'clock that morning, Poppy had to stock up the stationery cupboard. She was glad that she had to trek down to the floor below to get fresh supplies. Anything capable of taking her mind off the valentine card she had sent was welcome.

To say that she had got cold feet about that card would have been a major understatement. It had been an insane impulse and she hadn't stopped to think about what she'd been doing. Suspecting that Santino could hardly be looking forward to the staff party when it would only remind him of his father's sudden demise at Christmas, she had overflowed with sympathy for, as far as she knew, Santino had no other close relatives. And although her own family were still alive, they had emigrated to Australia and she rarely heard from them.

Even so, her far-too-emotional frame of mind the night before last was no excuse for the personal message she had inscribed on that card. She also had the sinking suspicion that Santino, who was the very image of ruthless workplace cool and efficiency, might very much have disliked receiving a huge pink envelope at the office. Surely some of the executive staff must have commented on that bright envelope? And possibly laughed, which was not something she felt that Santino would have enjoyed either.

That idiotic declaration of love had been her biggest misjudgement of all. Why had she let herself get so carried away? Why hadn't she had the wit to just sign it with only a question

mark? Then the card might have been interpreted in a dozen
ways and even as a harmless joke. But her statement of undying
love had put that crazy card into an entirely different realm and
might well rouse much greater curiosity.

Clutching a sheaf of paper and several bags of pens, Poppy
headed back towards the lift, her steps slowing when she saw
Santino chatting to several other men in the reception area. Her
heartbeat quickened, her chest tightened, her mouth ran dry,
symptoms that always assailed her when Santino Aragone was
in view or even within hearing. The dark, deep timbre of his
honeyed, accented drawl sent a positive tingle down her back-
bone. Santino could voice the most prosaic statistics and make
them sound like poetry.

While pretending great interest in the supplies she was carrying, Poppy glanced up and stole a look at him. *Bang*...the full
effect of Santino just exploded on her. She was entranced by
the commanding angle of his dark head, the gloss of his black
hair beneath the lights, the sheer height and breadth of him in a
dark formal business suit that exuded classic designer tailoring.
Yet when he moved he was as fluid as a big cat, and as graceful.
As he turned his head to address someone she caught his profile,
strong and distinctive from his lean, sculpted cheekbones to the
proud jut of his nose and the aggressive angle of his jawline.
His golden skin was stretched taut over his superb bone
structure.

He made her ache. Just looking at Santino made her ache. As
one of the bags of pens escaped the damp clutch of her nerveless
fingers and fell to the floor Santino swung round and she collided with his incredible eyes, black as sloes below these harsh
interior lights but the same shade as polished bronze in daylight.
His gaze narrowed, spiky black lashes curling down to zero in
on her. Then, instead of looking away again as she expected, he
stared almost as if he had never seen her before.

It was as if time stopped dead for Poppy. Her heart was pump-
ing blood so hard, she was as out of breath as if she had been
running. There was a singing sound in her eardrums and her
whole body felt oddly light and full of leaping energy. She
looked back at him, wide, very blue eyes steady for possibly the

very first time, and sank without trace in the glittering golden intensity of his appraisal.

Someone stooped and swept up the bag she had let fall, blocking her from Santino's gaze and breaking that spell. She focused with dizzy uncertainty on Craig Belston, absorbed the sneer etched on his self-satisfied features and almost recoiled, her fair skin reddening.

'You're making a patsy of yourself,' Craig murmured very low. 'The old dropped hanky routine went out with the ark!'

Her face tightened in shaken disconcertion. 'Sorry?'

Faint colour demarcating the hard slant of his cheekbones, Santino strode into the lift, hit the button to close the doors and left all his companions behind without even thinking about it. Poppy Bishop's hair was a vibrant golden auburn and very unusual. Just for a moment under the lights her hair had looked quite dazzling and she had beautiful eyes. For once, although he was quite certain that it would have been something that would have jarred on him, he had not noticed what she was wearing. But he was not attracted to her; of course, he wasn't.

Poppy was an employee, he reminded himself with relief. Not even if Cleopatra joined the staff would Santino have allowed himself to be tempted into an unsuitable liaison. That stupid card was still on his mind, that was all! He began with cool logic to list all Poppy's flaws. She was only about five feet three and he preferred tall blondes. She was twenty-one and he liked women closer to his own age. She had such dreadful dress sense that she stuck out like a canary bird among the suits at a meeting. She talked too much, knocked things over, messed up royally on the computer on a regular basis. He was a technical whizz, a perfectionist, she was an accident that just kept on happening. She was also the kind of woman men married and he would die single. The prospect of the funeral he had to attend that afternoon was stressing him out. What he ought to have was a drink.

Poppy hurried back to the marketing department and went to fetch Desmond's coffee. She was in turmoil. Why had Santino stared at her that way? Or had that just been her imagination? She was so ridiculously obsessed with him that her mind had probably played tricks on her. Why had she got this horrible suspicion that he knew she had sent that card? How could he *possibly* know? He couldn't read minds, could he?

And why had Craig attacked her that way when he usually behaved as though she was beneath his lofty notice? For goodness' sake, what had got into him? Craig Belston never deigned to speak to her, at least not since that first week when he had asked her out and badgered her to the point where she had been tactless enough to say that she had been warned about him. 'The old dropped hanky routine'? Did Craig suspect her feelings for Santino? But how could he?

It was madness to let her discomfiture about that wretched card work her up into a state, Poppy told herself in annoyance. Short of dusting the card for fingerprints and matching them to hers, there was no way that anyone could identify the sender. As for Craig, well, he had few friends at Aragone Systems and was pleasant to even fewer. Brainy he might be, but he had a nasty tongue and a habit of smirking at other people's misfortunes. So it would be foolish to read anything into those snide comments of his... Wouldn't it?

CHAPTER TWO

'NO...NO...NO!' Desmond urged Poppy in loud dismay. 'Just leave the coffee over there. I prefer to stretch my arm out!'

Although Poppy smiled like a good sport at the tide of amusement that those pointed instructions roused, she was cut to the bone. Hadn't she suffered enough yet for the episode of the spilt coffee? A lecture about safety measures with liquids from the HR manager had set the seal on her shame while she had also been reminded of her first formal warning, which had resulted from poor timekeeping in her very first month at Aragone Systems. 'One more strike and you're out,' had been the message she'd received after the coffee incident and she really was determined not to make any further blunders.

'What are you wearing to the party tonight?'

Grateful for the interruption, Poppy glanced up with a smile from the unexciting graph she had been tinkering with on her monitor. It was Lesley, a tall, slim brunette on the market research team. 'Nothing special. Just a dress.'

She listened while Lesley described her own outfit. She knew that without a doubt it would enhance every slender curve of the other woman's enviable figure. As Desmond informed her that he wanted the graphs she had been working on for a meeting, she hurried into printing them, relieved that she had finished the last one in time.

'I heard that Santino got a valentine card,' Lesley continued, and as Poppy tensed she added, 'I was more surprised to hear he didn't get a whole sackful! I bet it was from his ex trying to get back in with him.'

'Ex?' Poppy queried, relaxing again.

'Don't you read the gossip columns? He dumped Caro Hartley a month back,' Lesley informed her with authority. 'I didn't think that would last long. She's quite a party girl and I suspect Santino got bored fast. He's a very clever guy.'

'I'm sure he'll not be on his own for long,' Poppy remarked, anxious eyes on Desmond, her boss, as he treated the printed graphs to a cursory appraisal. Had she changed the colouring of the one she had first done in pink for her own amusement? Yes, she was sure she remembered doing so. Even so, she didn't lose her tension until he had slotted them into a folder.

Never, ever again would she play around with the colours of the graphs, she swore as she went into the cloakroom to freshen up at lunchtime. If it killed her, she was going to erase her every bad habit. She gave herself only the most fleeting look in the mirror. At least she had grown out of the spots and her skin now looked great. But her rippling auburn curls were a constant source of aggravation, for the little tendrils that gathered round her face ensured that her hair never looked as tidy as other women's. However, cut short her riotous curls were even harder to handle, so she kept her hair long and wore it clipped back at the nape of her neck.

Her unfashionable curves were the biggest challenge, she conceded ruefully. She was in dire need of a new, inspiring diet. The banana regime had put her off bananas for life, and the cabbage soup one had ensured that she felt queasy just passing vegetables on a market stall. No, it was back to boring old salad and yogurt, which worked but meant that she spent most of her time fantasising about food and feeling so hungry she could have munched on wood.

When she returned to her desk, the email icon was flicking on her monitor and she opened it, hoping it was a cheering communication from a friend.

'Pink graphs are inappropriate in a business environment,' ran the email.

Poppy looked at the message in shock and then glanced around herself to see if anyone was looking at her, but nobody was. Who had seen her mucking about with that graph before lunch? Who was pulling her leg? It was unsigned and the address was a six-digit number and, as such, anonymous.

'Says who?' she typed in and sent the email back.

'I like graphs in dark colours.'

'That's boring,' Poppy told her correspondent.

'Rational. Pink is a distraction.'

'Pink is warm and uplifting,' she protested in reply, typing at full tilt.

'Pink is irritating, cute, feminine…inappropriate.' That awful word, inappropriate again. Her correspondent was a guy, she decided, and certainly not Desmond, who regarded email as a time-wasting exercise and who would surely have gone into orbit the instant he saw a pink graph.

'How did you see my graph?' she typed.

'Stick to the issue.'

Poppy grinned at that rejoinder. *Definitely* a guy.

'One more warning and you could be out of work. Be sensible.' That next message came in fast on the previous one without having given her the chance to respond.

Her grin fell off her lips at supersonic speed. 'How do you know that?' she typed.

But this time, infuriatingly, there was no answer. Thinking about her mystery correspondent, Poppy conceded that quite a few people would be aware of those warnings on her employment record. The very first time it had happened she had been so upset, she had talked about it herself and, after the coffee episode, Desmond had been so furious that he had announced his intent to complain about her in such ringing decibels that most of the department had heard him.

Intrigued by those emails, scanning her busy colleagues with intense curiosity, Poppy sent several more to the same address that afternoon but still received no further response. Then she began thinking about the party that evening and wondered what she would wear, since pink had become such a controversial issue…

'I'm *amazed* that you're still laying on large supplies of alcohol for your employees.' Jenna Delsen's exquisite face emanated shocked disapproval as she scanned the low-lit noisy room full of party revellers. 'Daddy used to help our staff to get sloshed at our expense, too, but not since *I* joined the company. Now we have a nice sober supper do. No loud music, no dancing, no drink and everyone behaves.'

'I like my staff to enjoy themselves. It is only one night a year.' Santino suppressed the ungenerous thought that the blonde could be a pious, penny-pinching misery, for she had been welcome company at the funeral that afternoon and he had enjoyed dining with her and her father at their home afterwards.

'I suppose that's the extrovert Italian in you. You threw some very riotous parties when we were at Oxford together.' Jenna gave him a flirtatious, rather coy look as she reminded him that they had known each other since university.

In receipt of that appraisal, all Santino's defensive antenna hit alarm status. 'Let me get you a drink,' he suggested faster than the speed of light, already mentally listing the unattached executives present on the slender but hopeful thought that she might take a shine to one of them instead. They had always been friends, *never* anything else.

Jenna curved a slender hand round his arm when he returned to her side. 'I have a confession to make…for the whole of the time we were at uni together, I was in love with you.'

Santino conceded that what had started out as an unusual day, and had gravitated into being a very long day, was now assuming nightmarish proportions. 'You're kidding me.'

'No.' Jenna fixed her very fine green eyes on him in speaking condemnation. 'And you never noticed. In four *long* years, you never once noticed that I felt rather more for you than the average mate.'

In one unappreciative gulp, Santino tipped back an entire shot of brandy meant to be savoured at leisure. He was transfixed and trapped by that censorious speech. There was no polite or kind way of telling her that, beautiful and intellectually challenging as she was—for she had a first-class brain—there had been no spark whatsoever on his side of the fence.

'And I had to sit back and watch you chasing girls who couldn't hold a candle to me,' Jenna continued with withering bite.

'Oddly enough, I don't recall you sitting home alone many nights,' Santino countered sardonically.

'Once I understood that I was in love with a commitment-phobe, I trained myself to regard you only as a friend—'

'Jenna…when you first met me, I was eighteen. Most teenage boys are commitment-phobes.' Santino groaned, thinking what an absolute pain she seemed to have become, still nourishing her sense of injustice over the unwitting blow he had dealt to her ego so many years after the event. 'I was no better and no worse than most—'

'Oh, don't be so modest,' Jenna trilled in sharp interruption. 'All the girls were crazy about you! You were spoilt for choice but you deliberately chose women whom you knew would only be short-term distractions. You always protected yourself from the threat of a steady relationship and you're *still* doing it!'

When Santino went back to the bar for another drink, Jenna was so taken up with her discourse that she accompanied him. Santino's temper was on a very short leash and his second drink went the way of the first. He was cursing the innate good manners that had persuaded him that he ought to invite the blonde to accompany him to the party. He was thinking of what a very much better time he would have had mixing with his staff. Then he glanced across the room and saw a figure hovering in the doorway and the remainder of Jenna's barbed criticisms washed off him because he no longer heard them.

Noticing that she had lost his attention, Jenna followed the direction of his gaze. She saw a youthful redhead with a vibrant mane of curly hair. Small, very pretty, but not at all Santino's style. Yet Santino was so busy watching the girl that he had forgotten Jenna was there.

Scanning the crowded room, Poppy finally picked out Lesley in her distinctive white and silver dress and began to move towards her, an apologetic smile on her lips. She was a little late but then some of her colleagues had opted to stay on in the city centre and warm up in a bar before attending the party. But Poppy loved getting ready to go out at home and had known that she didn't have enough of a head for drink to have sustained a lengthy pre-party session.

'I really like that dress,' Lesley said warmly as she flipped out a seat for Poppy's occupation. 'Where did you buy it?'

'It's not new. I got it for my brother's wedding,' Poppy confided, and then added in an undertone. 'To be honest, it's my bridesmaid's dress—'

'I wish my best friend had let me wear an outfit like that for her big day. At least I could have worn it again afterwards.' Lesley admired the strappy green dress that flattered Poppy's shapely figure and slim length of leg, then drew Poppy's attention to the drinks already lined up in readiness for her, pointing out that she was very much behind the rest of them, before continuing, 'It must have been an unusual wedding.'

'My sister-in-law, Karrie, wanted a casual evening do. She wore a short dress, too.'

Poppy's attention, which had been automatically roaming the room in search of a certain tall, dark male, finally found Santino where he stood by the bar with a spectacular blonde woman clinging to his arm. She lifted the drink that Lesley had nudged into her fingers and sipped it to ease her tight throat, but she resisted the urge to ask the chatty brunette if she knew who Santino's companion was. After all, what was the point? Did it make any difference who it was? And it was none of her business either.

Indeed, she should not even be *looking* at Santino Aragone, Poppy told herself guiltily, because looking was only feeding her obsession. Having thought over Craig's sneering remarks earlier that day, Poppy had finally faced the unhappy fact that he at least suspected that she was rather too attached to their mutual employer. That conclusion had unnerved her for Craig's reputation for making others the butt of his cruel sense of humour was well-known. So, she would have to be more circumspect in the future, for languishing like a lovelorn teenager over Santino could easily make her a laughing stock at work. In fact, she would be much better devoting her brain to sussing out the mystery identity of her email correspondent, who had to at least *like* her to have gone to the trouble of trying to give her a warning word of advice, she reflected.

'Who is she?' Jenna enquired very drily of Santino.

'Who are you talking about?' Santino asked with a magnificent disregard for the direction of his own gaze.

'The little redhead with the pre-Raphaelite hair...the one

whom you've been watching for at least *three solid minutes*,' Jenna completed between gritted teeth.

'I'm not watching her,' Santino murmured with cool disdain.

'But even though you employ hundreds of young women you know *instantly* who I'm referring to,' Jenna noted with rapier-sharp feminine logic.

'Did you get out of the wrong side of the bed this morning?' Santino drawled with his sudden flashing smile. 'Exactly *why* are you trying to wind me up?'

'Before I tell you—' Jenna gave him a grudging smile of approbation for finally registering that she had been set on evening the score for past injuries '—you tell me who the redhead is and I will give you ten very good reasons why one should never, ever date an employee.'

Santino drained his drink again and dealt her a mocking glance. 'I don't need them, Jenna. All ten of them are in my mind right now.'

Returning to her table after chatting to various friends, Poppy sat down again. Lesley and two other women were chatting about Santino's date, who was evidently the daughter of the owner of Delsen Industries.

'What do *you* think of Jenna?' another, less welcome voice enquired.

Poppy's head swivelled, her startled gaze only then registering that Craig Belston had joined their table during her absence. That question had been directed specifically at her and she was gripped by discomfiture. 'Why would I think anything of her?' she answered with a determined smile. 'All the boss's girlfriends are incredible beauties.'

'Now why did I get the idea that you mightn't have noticed that?' Craig rested his pale blue probing eyes on Poppy and her mouth ran dry.

'Santino's leggy ladies are rather hard to miss.' Lesley shot a frowning glance at Santino's PA and added, 'Come on. You've been keeping us all in suspense since we finished work. Who sent Santino the naff card?'

Poppy froze and then gulped down her drink as her colour heightened.

'Did I mention that it was an *inside* job?' Craig murmured with tormenting slowness and Poppy's heart skipped an entire beat, her every tiny muscle pulling rigid.

'No, you darned well didn't!' one of the other women piped up in exasperation. 'Who on earth working for Santino would be daft enough to send him a valentine card swearing undying love? I mean, come on, *yes*, he's hugely fanciable, but he's the last guy around who would respond to that kind of blatant invitation from a member of staff.'

'You said the card wasn't signed,' Lesley reminded Craig. 'So how could you know it was sent by someone in Aragone Systems? It didn't come through the internal mail, did it?'

'Just assume that in this particular case we're talking about someone who's not very bright,' Craig invited, and Poppy's tummy began to churn where she sat. 'Someone who assumed that only a name would expose her identity.'

'You recognised the handwriting!' someone exclaimed.

'I really don't think I like this conversation very much,' Lesley remarked suddenly. 'Valentine cards are just for fun.'

'It wasn't the handwriting. It was a combination of errors,' Craig explained to the table at large. 'A distinctive perfume, a predilection for a particular colour and a love of flowers.'

Poppy was now as pale as milk and feeling physically ill with humiliation. She could not bring herself to look at any of her companions and silence greeted Craig's last explanation, an awful uneasy silence that left Poppy's nerves screaming and her skin clammy.

'Now who do we all know who wears jasmine scent?' Craig murmured.

'I don't know anyone who wears that,' Lesley chimed in, and the two other women followed her lead to say the exact same. Painfully conscious that her companions were trying to throw sand in Craig's eyes and deflect him from his target, Poppy had to grit her teeth to prevent herself from lifting her drink and throwing it at her tormentor.

At the other side of the room, Jenna was still in full confiding mode, but Santino was having a hard time dragging his brooding scrutiny from his PA's smug expression and Poppy's pale, rigid face.

'So, I hope you'll forgive me for giving you a rough time tonight,' Jenna murmured in dulcet continuation, 'but I always promised myself that some day I would tell you the truth and make you sweat for a few minutes. Will you still come to my engagement party?'

Taken aback, Santino frowned. '*Engagement* party?'

'I'm so grateful I'm not in love with you any more.' Jenna sighed. 'Didn't you hear me telling you that I'm getting engaged to David Marsh and that he's picking me up here in five minutes?'

It had been a long time since Santino had heard that much good news in one sentence; he was genuinely fond of Jenna and relief on his own behalf and pleasure on her behalf sliced through his growing tension. Realising that the blonde had merely been set on claiming a small slice of revenge for his past indifference to her, he flung back his handsome dark head and started to laugh with genuine appreciation.

The sight of Santino splitting his sides with laughter, and Jenna equally convulsed and holding onto him for support, filled Poppy with paranoia. Immediately, she assumed that Santino had told the blonde about her pathetic card and that they were laughing at her, for if Craig had guessed that she was the culprit he was certain to have told Santino. Feeling as if she had just had her heart ripped out while she was still breathing, Poppy nonetheless rose from her seat with as much dignity as she could muster, for she could not bear sitting there playing poor little victim for Craig's benefit any longer.

'You're a real Sherlock Holmes, Craig,' she said flatly. 'I'm very impressed.'

Poppy walked away fast. Tears were stinging her eyes and blurring her vision, but she kept her head high and that was her final undoing. She didn't see the small table laden with drinks in her path. She hit it with such force that the table tipped over with an enormous crash that seemed to turn every head in the room. For an instant, Poppy hovered, staring in horror at the smashed glass and liquid everywhere, not to mention the startled dancers leaping back from the mess she had created. Then her control just snapped and she fled.

'Now,' Lesley said icily to Craig, who was sniggering at Poppy's noisy exit, 'while you're wondering why Poppy's friends aren't rushing after her to offer support, watch Santino and *learn*…'

'What are you talking about?'

'Upsetting Poppy is not a career-enhancing move in Aragone Systems. You see, if you were a woman and in touch with the *real* newsbreaking gossip in this building, you would already *know* that Santino fancies the socks off Poppy, too—'

'Rubbish!' Craig snapped. 'He binned the card!'

'Did you check the bin at the end of the day?' someone enquired drily.

'Santino doesn't know what's hit him yet,' one of the other women commented with immense superiority. 'He's more at home with his keyboard than his emotions.'

'But when a bloke like Santino, who likes everything done by the book, starts telling poor Desmond that pink graphs are fresh and creative, he's in *very* deep,' Lesley completed.

In companionable and expectant silence, the three women then focused pointedly on Santino, who had stridden forward the instant that Poppy had sent the table flying. He swung round to speak to Jenna Delsen and not thirty seconds later left in the same direction as Poppy. Witnessing that demonstration, Craig turned the greyish colour of putty and groaned out loud.

CHAPTER THREE

WHEN Poppy emerged from the function room at full tilt, several women were entering the cloakroom across the foyer and she wheeled away in the opposite direction.

Finding herself by the lifts, she stabbed the call button with a frantic hand and gulped back a sob. She had to find a quiet corner to pull herself back together again. Selecting the marketing floor, she slumped back against the lift's cold steel wall as the doors closed. Wrapping her arms round herself, she hugged herself tight. But it was no help, no comfort, because all she could think about was what a fool she had made of herself.

When she saw the dark reception area on the marketing floor, it looked eerie and she hit the door button again in a hurry and tried another floor. Her eyes flooded with burning tears. Of course, Santino Aragone would have laughed when he was told who had sent that card. Everybody would be laughing! After all, she was just a junior member of staff, the plump little redhead Craig had nastily labelled, 'Tinkerbell' and hardly competition for the gorgeous women Santino specialised in. Why on earth hadn't common sense intervened before she'd posted that stupid card to Santino at the office? Didn't she *have* sense like other people? Her throat aching, she could no longer hold back the tears and a sob escaped her. How could she have exposed herself to that extent?

In the foyer below, Santino was watching the lights that indicated which floor the lift was at. The light flicked through the levels in descent again, made several brief stops and then sank as low as the floor above before beginning to ascend again. When the lift finally reached the executive level, he waited in taut suspense to see if it moved on again.

When the doors opened on the top floor, Poppy blinked in confusion for she had lost track. But low lights were burning and the floor was not in darkness like the others. Dimly recalling

25

that Santino's secretary had a private washroom, Poppy stumbled out. She needed to tidy herself up and fix her face before she could go home.

But shock was still setting in hard on Poppy. Only when it was far too late to change things did she see her mistake. She *should* have toughed out Craig's insinuations. Instead she had fallen right into his trap and confirmed his suspicions. He couldn't have proved anything, yet she had virtually confessed by saying what she had and leaving the table.

Taunting, wounding images were now bombarding her mind, increasing her distress. She had left the party with all the cool of a baby elephant let loose in a drawing room. She saw Craig's self-satisfied smile, Santino laughing, the stiff, disapproving faces of the other women. Craig might as well have stripped her naked in public. Her trembling hands braced on the edge of the washroom vanity unit and, letting her head hang for she couldn't stand to look at herself in the mirror when she hated herself so much for her own stupidity, she began to sob.

Santino had never made it from the lift to his secretary's office so fast. But then those heartbreaking sobs acted on him like a shriek alarm. He would usually have gone quite some distance to avoid a crying woman, but the curious automatic pilot now overruling his normal caution ensured that he strode right through the open door of the washroom and gathered Poppy straight into a comforting embrace.

The sheer shock value of a pair of masculine arms closing round her when she had believed that she was alone provoked a startled cry from Poppy. Then she looked up and focused on Santino and even more shock froze her from head to toe. Bronze-coloured eyes set below lush black lashes were trained to hers, the lean, dark contours of his handsome features taut with concern.

'It's OK,' he soothed in his gorgeous accented drawl.

'Is it?' Poppy's voice emerged on the back of a breathless sob, for she could not have got oxygen into her lungs at that instant had her life depended on it. What was happening should have felt unreal but, in actuality, being in the circle of Santino's arms felt very real and very right. Furthermore, it was something she had been dreaming of for so long that no power on earth could have sent her into retreat.

'Course it is,' Santino asserted, not really knowing what he was talking about, then deciding it was safer to confine himself to inconsequentials rather than risk reawakening her distress. Lifting a lean hand, he curved it round the back of her head to urge her face back into his shoulder where she had started out.

Poppy's tension evaporated and she subsided against him, feeling as boneless as a rag doll. The faint aroma of whatever shaving lotion he used assailed her and immediately became familiar to her: rather exotic, distinctively male. She sucked in a steadying breath, her fingers resting lightly against his broad shoulder, yet she could still feel the flex of his lean, powerful muscles beneath the expensive cloth of his jacket as he held her close. He could be so kind. How had she managed to forget how considerate he had been when she had hurt her finger and he had taken her to hospital? A little calmer, better able to think than she had been minutes earlier at the height of her distress, she saw how unlikely it was that Santino had been nastily indulging in a good laugh at her expense with his ladyfriend. He wasn't like that.

'Let's get out of here,' Santino urged with a faint quiver of wry amusement edging his deep voice. 'This is my secretary's inner sanctum and I feel like an intruder.'

In a jerky motion, she peeled herself from him again, her colour high, her eyes lowering, for she was sure she looked a total fright after giving way to all those tears. Her nose would be pink, her eyes swollen and her mascara might have run. Not that she felt that he would care either way, but she didn't want him seeing her at her very worst. He pressed a light hand to her tense spine and turned her back into the office beyond and on into what had to be his own office.

Abandoning her in the centre of the dark room, Santino strode over to the desk to switch on the light there and indicated a door to her left. 'You can freshen up in there if you like.'

Her eyes widened at the sight of the big luxurious office and then centred back on Santino where he was poised by his desk. The pool of illumination shed by the lamp shrank the large room to more cosy contours but simply emphasised his impact. He was so tall, so wonderfully dark and vibrant. Why was it that every time she looked at Santino he seemed more gorgeous than ever? As she encountered the onslaught of his mesmeric dark golden eyes her heartbeat thudded in what felt like the foot of her throat. She reddened, suddenly all too conscious of the emotions that had got her into such a mess in the first place. Dropping her head again, she went through the door he had indicated.

Santino released his breath in a slow, sustained hiss. He would chat to her for a while just to smooth matters over and then tuck her into a taxi to go home. Concerned employer? He grimaced, picturing her standing there in that green dress that defined her lush curves, the fiery luxuriance of her glorious hair tumbling round her face, bright blue eyes full of strain. He wanted to see her usual sunny smile replace that hunted look. He just liked her, that was all. There was nothing wrong with that that he could see.

Poppy winced when she saw her tousled reflection in the mirror on the wall of Santino's opulent washroom. Breathing in deep because her head was swimming a little, she repaired her eye make-up but didn't bother to refresh her lipstick, lest he think that she was getting tarted up for his benefit. Don't think about that valentine card, she warned herself fiercely. What was done was done and, whether he knew she had penned that card or not, he was hardly likely to mention it. Having dried her hands, she emerged again.

'Take a seat,' Santino told her.

'Don't you have to get back to the party?'

'No. I don't usually stay to the bitter end. My presence tends to inhibit people,' Santino advanced with a wry smile that lent his lean, dark face such innate charm that for several tense seconds she simply couldn't take her eyes from him. 'Would you like a drink?'

'What have you got?'

'Just about everything,' Santino informed her, deadpan. 'Come and have a look…'

Madly self-conscious of her own every move, but enervated by the novel sensation of being alone with him, Poppy moved closer, peered into the packed drinks cabinet and opted for what she hoped was the most sophisticated choice. She backed away with the glass until her legs brushed the low arm of one of the comfortable leather sofas that filled one corner. She sat down on the arm, too skittish to seat herself in the more normal way.

She watched him pour a brandy from a cut-crystal decanter, light burnishing his black hair, accentuating his hard cheekbones and the very faint blue cast of stubble already shadowing his strong jawline. She hadn't seen him when he needed a shave before and she decided that it gave him a very sexy, macho look. As he straightened he shot a glance at her and caught her staring.

'So,' Santino murmured on a casual note intended to put her at her ease. 'Where did you work before you came here?'

'I was a nanny…that's what I trained for when I left school,' Poppy advanced, her face flushed, her voice tense as she strove to match his relaxation.

'A nanny.' Santino was initially surprised and then he saw her in his mind's eye surrounded by a bunch of children and it was like the missing piece of a jigsaw puzzle suddenly sliding into place for him. Kids would adore her, he thought. She would throw herself into their games, never mind when they got dirty, fuss over them and hug them when they got hurt. Thinking of the chilly, correct sourpuss of a nanny he had had to endure as a little boy, he felt positively deprived.

'How come you ended up in Aragone Systems?' Santino prompted.

Poppy sighed. 'My first placement was with a diplomat's family and I was with them for two whole years…'

'Did they make you work endless hours for a pittance?' Santino enquired cynically.

A brief smile blossomed on her lips at that idea. 'No, they were a lovely family. They treated me very well. The problem was all mine. I got far too attached to the children and when they left England and I was no longer needed, I was just devastated,' she admitted ruefully. 'So I decided it wasn't the job for me and signed up for an office skills course.'

Within an ace of remarking that he considered that decision

a wrong move on her part, Santino thought better of it when he registered that he could not imagine the marketing department without her.

'The trouble is…the career change hasn't worked out very well,' Poppy commented rather gruffly.

Santino's ebony brows pleated. 'Everyone makes an occasional mistake—'

'I've managed to pick up two formal warnings in six months.' Poppy shrugged a slight shoulder, cursing her own impulsive tongue, her habit of being too candid for other people's comfort. All she had done was bring her own failings to his notice.

Santino had to resist a strong but unprofessional urge to tell her that her head of department had been guilty of an over-reaction when he'd made a complaint about her on the strength of an accident with a spilt drink. She had been unlucky. Desmond Lines was in his first week in the job, keen to make his mark and show his authority, but he had chosen the wrong event and the wrong person to clamp down on. In fact, Poppy might not know it, but that misjudged warning had even been discussed in the boardroom with varying degrees of levity and incredulity. One of Santino's senior executives had looked in mock horror at the puddle of mineral water he had left on the table and had wondered out loud if HR were going to haul him over the coals, too.

Poppy tilted her chin. 'I didn't make mistakes as a nanny.'

'But people would miss you if you weren't here.'

Colliding with glittering dark golden eyes, Poppy felt dizzy. Did he mean *he* would miss her? For goodness' sake, what was she thinking? What difference would it make to him if she went off in search of another job and moved on? She was one very humble cog in a big wheel. He was just being kind again.

Quick to recognise when a subject ought to be changed, Santino asked, 'Do you have any family living in London?'

Poppy moistened her dry lips with her drink and sighed, 'Not any more. My parents moved out to Australia about eighteen months back. My brother, Peter, and his wife, Karrie, live in Sydney.'

'What's the connection that took them all to the other side of the world?' Santino enquired lazily, lounging back with indolent elegance against the edge of his desk.

'Basically…Peter. He's married to an Australian and he was offered a very prestigious teaching post at a university out there. He's a brilliant mathematician. He was doing algebra as a toddler.' A self-deprecating smile curved Poppy's lips. 'I was still struggling to do it at twelve years old.'

'There are more important things,' Santino quipped, opting for the sympathy vote and overlooking his own stratospheric success in the same subject. 'So why didn't you emigrate to Australia with your family?'

'Well…I wasn't *asked*,' Poppy confided with a rueful grin of acknowledgement at that oversight. 'Mum and Dad just worship the ground Peter walks on. They've bought a retirement home near where he and Karrie live. Mum now looks after their house and Dad keeps their garden blooming.'

'Free labour…not bad if you can get it. Does your sister-in-law mind?'

'Not at all. Karrie's a doctor and works very long hours. She's also now expecting their first child. As an arrangement, it suits them all very well.'

'Do you have any other relatives left in the U.K.?' Santino pressed with a frown.

'An elderly great-aunt in Wales whom I visit for the odd weekend. What about you?' Poppy questioned, emboldened by that dialogue.

'Me?'

'I suppose that if you have any relatives they live in Italy,' Poppy answered for herself. 'When did your mother die?'

Santino tensed, his jawline clenching. 'She's not dead. My parents were divorced.'

Disconcerted, Poppy nodded, thinking that that was a little known fact in Aragone Systems for most people had assumed that Maximo Aragone had been a widower.

Santino drained his glass and set it down. 'I haven't seen my mother since I was fifteen.'

'How *awful*!' Poppy exclaimed, her soft heart going out to

him at the thought that he had been abandoned by some hard-hearted woman.

Santino shot her a look of surprise and then added drily, 'It was *my* choice to cut her out of my life.'

At that explanation, Poppy surveyed him in sincere shock, and when he went on with complete cool to ask her if she wanted another drink, she said no. Although she suspected that what he had just confided was rather private, she could not rest without knowing more.

'Was your mother cruel to you?' Poppy asked baldly.

'Of course not. She loved me very much but she was not such a good wife to my father,' Santino advanced on a forbidding note that would have warned the more cautious off the topic.

'Oh…I see. You took your *father's* side when they divorced.' Poppy spoke that thought out loud without meaning to.

Raw exasperation currented through Santino. As if it were that simple! As if it weren't possible that he had reached such a decision on the strength of his own judgement!

The silence seethed.

Recognising that she had got too personal, Poppy turned pink with discomfiture. 'I'm sorry. It's just…you said she loved you and yet you've been *so* cruel to her.' As she registered what she had said she actually clamped a sealing hand over her parted lips and surveyed Santino's set features and flaring golden eyes in dismay and apology. 'It's time I tucked my big mouth up for the night,' she muttered through her spread fingers.

'No…I will defend myself against that charge first!' Santino countered forcefully. 'Let me tell you why I hate St Valentine's Day…'

'You…*do*?' Her hand falling back to her lap, Poppy stared at him in a combination of surprise and confusion.

'I adored my mother,' Santino grated. 'So did my father. He flew her over to Paris to her favourite hotel to celebrate St Valentine's Day and do you know what *she* did?'

In silence and very much wishing she had minded her own business, Poppy shook her curly head.

'That's the night she chose to tell him she'd been having an affair and that she was leaving him for her lover!' Santino ground out like an Old Testament prophet reading out the Riot Act, raw censure in every hard male angle of his striking features.

Poppy pondered that explanation. 'She probably felt so guilty that she couldn't help confessing…I bet she didn't choose that night or those circumstances deliberately.'

'Whatever…Maximo was *shattered*,' Santino stressed on a note of decided finality.

'Was he…?' Poppy compressed her lips on the question she was dying to ask, but then discovered that she was unable to hold it in. 'Was he always faithful to her?'

It was an issue that Santino had never before discussed and she was coming back at him on an angle he had actually never once considered. He stilled in angry unease, looked at Poppy's intent face and wondered why the hell he was suffering from a sudden need to justify a decision he had not once wavered from in fifteen years. It had been that little word 'cruel' that had shaken him, disturbed him in a way he could not have believed. Dark colour marked his superb cheekbones.

'You're not sure he was…are you?' Poppy whispered, recognising the rare flash of uncertainty now lightening Santino's dark gaze. 'Yet you still judged her and not him. But then I've heard that it can be harder for boys to forgive their mother's… er…mistakes.'

'Tinkerbell…the *oracle*?' Santino derided with all the cutting force of his own unsettled emotions. 'That's got to be a new one.'

Poppy flinched as though he had slapped her and every ounce of her natural colour drained away. He had never utilised that tone on her before, much less looked at her with a pure dismissive contempt that bit right through her tender skin to her bones and made her feel about an inch high. And, of course, he was right, for what did she know about such a situation? Some of her friends had lived through their parents' breaking up but she had no personal experience. Who was she to tell him that he had been unjust and cruel?

'You're right…' Her voice emerged slightly thickened by the stark rise of tears threatening her again and she slid off the arm of the sofa in a hurried movement. 'I can't even solve my own problems, much less tackle other people's. A-and as you've already said,' she stammered in growing desperation as she turned round in a blind uncoordinated circle, 'you don't have a problem in the first place—'

'I'm sorry,' Santino bit out in a rather raw undertone.

'Never mind. I'm hardly the world's most diplomatic person…especially after a few drinks,' Poppy mumbled, narrowly missing a sculpture on a pedestal in her haste to reach the door. 'Maybe I was even a bit jealous.'

'Jealous?' Santino echoed in incomprehension as he tracked her the whole way across his office.

'Yeah…' Poppy had to force herself to turn back. 'You said your mother loved you very much. If mine had ever loved me like that she might answer my letters more often.'

Santino groaned something in Italian and reached for her hands to prevent her from getting any closer to the door. 'Come here…' he urged thickly.

CHAPTER FOUR

SUDDENLY extraordinarily short of breath, Poppy stared up at Santino and as she met his beautiful dark golden eyes she drowned there in her own reflection.

Santino inched her steadily closer until bare inches separated them. 'I want to kiss you…'

'Seriously…?' Her wide gaze clung to his.

'I want to take you home to my bed,' Santino confessed raggedly. 'In fact, I can't think of anything else…'

Poppy blinked. It was as if a little buzzer went off in her brain and allowed her to think again. But what he was telling her was still such an enormous surprise, she just ended up staring up at him again, dark pupils dilated, moist lips parted on her own ragged breathing. He wanted to *kiss* her? That revelation wholly enchanted her. But the second was too much to handle for as yet no man had contrived to persuade Poppy either to go home with him or allow him to come home with her.

'But I'll settle for a kiss…and then supper somewhere public, *cara mia.*' Santino noted the sudden anxious expression in her gaze and the rise of colour in her cheeks with the strangest, newest sense of protectiveness he had ever experienced. He didn't know what he was doing and, for the first time in his very structured life, he realised that he didn't care.

Poppy's heart was playing leapfrog with her ribs. He was attracted to her, too? She couldn't believe it. She was achingly conscious of his hands holding hers and such a flood of happiness filled her that she felt literally light-headed with it and her throat ached. 'Kiss…' she selected her favourite option, the one she could least bear to wait for.

Santino smiled, his heartbreaking, stunning smile that lit up his vibrant bronzed features and sent her pulses racing. 'Only one kiss…otherwise I might not stop.'

'One's a bit mean,' Poppy argued. 'I've been waiting a long

time for this. Oh, good heavens, you've left your girlfriend downstairs!' she suddenly gasped, her expression one of comical horror.

'Jenna's just an old friend and she's already left,' Santino assured her with a laugh of appreciation.

As relief at that explanation travelled through Poppy, Santino was already drawing her back across the office towards the corner with the sofas. It was so cool and natural the way he did it, too, that she was helplessly impressed. She couldn't dredge her attention from his lean, strong face, couldn't quite accept that what was happening was really happening. Her legs went weak under her at just the thought of his wide, sensual mouth on hers and she was so keen for it to happen, she was ashamed of herself.

'What are you thinking about?' Santino murmured silkily.

'Kissing you…' Poppy told him, but in truth she was equally enthralled by the new and more intimate side of Santino that she was seeing. It occurred to her that he was in his element, she the one floundering and following his smooth, assured lead.

'Kissing me…' Santino repeated huskily as he tugged her down onto the sofa, wound long fingers through her hair, curving them to the nape of her neck to angle her mouth up to his.

'You're good at this,' Poppy muttered, trembling with the most wicked amount of anticipation.

'Ought to be…' Santino treated her to a slashing irreverent grin that acknowledged his own experience and her eyes clung to his lean, powerful face, her heart hammering. 'But I've never got this close to a woman in the office before—'

'No?'

'Feels forbidden and…*fantastic*,' Santino growled in a throaty purr of hunger.

Poppy quivered, every skincell leaping, and when he brought his mouth down on hers, when he hauled her close, fantastic was in her opinion a serious understatement. She fell into that explosive kiss as though she had been waiting all her life for it.

He captured her lips with intoxicating urgency and with sensual slowness let his tongue slide into her mouth in a darting, probing invasion that was unbelievably exciting. Poppy had never felt what she felt then, not that rise of inner heat or that sudden charged impatience for more that gripped her like a greedy vice. She couldn't get enough of his hot, hard mouth. Every so often sheer necessity forced them to break off just to breathe but they welded back together again fast, Santino groaning low in his throat and muttering fiercely against her swollen mouth, 'You blow me away, *cara*.'

He pulled back from her to shrug free of his suit jacket and wrench at his silk tie to loosen his shirt collar. Sucking in a shallow, shaken breath, Poppy slumped weak as water back against the arm of the sofa and just watched him. The tie was discarded on the carpet beside his jacket and as he straightened he swept her ankles up so that she was lying full length. He slid off her shoes and let them drop as well. Poppy collided with smouldering dark golden eyes and she had never been so electrified with sheer excitement in her entire life.

Santino ran deceptively indolent eyes over her as she lay there all of a quiver, his attention lingering with potent appreciation on her. 'I love your hair…it's incredible and you've got a very, very sexy mouth…'

'Don't stop talking,' Poppy whispered helplessly.

'If I talk, I can't kiss you,' Santino pointed out thickly, scanning her feminine curves in a more bold and intimate appraisal that sent the blood drumming at an insane rate through her veins.

'Problem,' she agreed, barely able to squeeze that single word out.

'Not an impossible one, *cara*,' Santino assured her in his wicked dark drawl, his intense bronzed eyes signalling pure enticement and sensual promise. 'I can think of several very interesting pursuits that I can talk through.'

The atmosphere sizzled. His smile flashed out once more and she just ached so much for contact again that she sat up, grabbed his shoulder to steady herself and found his passionate mouth again for herself. A low moan of response was wrenched from her as he suckled at her lips and then parted them to invade her mouth again.

'Thought I had to talk,' Santino teased as he lowered her back to the sofa and unbuttoned the rest of his shirt.

'No...' Her mouth ran dry as she stared up at him. He looked
so big and powerful. A haze of short dark curls delineated his
broad, muscular chest and his skin was the vibrant colour of
bronze. Her body tensed, wild heat snaking up inside her again.

'Last time I was on a sofa with a female, I was sixteen,'
Santino confided with dancing amusement in his dark golden
gaze.

He lifted her up to him with easy strength and curved her
round him. Cool air hit her taut spine as he unzipped her dress.
He brushed down the delicate straps on her slim shoulders and
released his breath in a slow, sexy hiss of appreciation as he
bared her lush, pouting breasts.

'Superb...every inch of you is a work of art, *cara mia*,'
Santino swore with husky fervour as a tide of shy pink washed
up into her cheeks. 'Without a doubt you are the perfect reward
at the end of a lousy day.'

Then he touched her and she was immediately lost in the
passion again. All control was wrested from her by the seductive
delight of his skilled fingers on her tender flesh and the even
more intense excitement of his knowing mouth caressing the
almost painfully sensitive rosy peaks. With a whimper of tor-
mented response, she surrendered to that world of wild
sensation...

CHAPTER FIVE

SANTINO wakened to the buzz of his mobile phone.

Disorientated in a way that was far from being the norm for him, he sat up, realised that he was still in the office and dug into his jacket for his phone. It was a very apologetic security guard calling up from the ground floor to ask if he was still upstairs working. *Working?* Santino stole a lingering glance at Poppy where she lay fast asleep beneath the suit jacket in which he had rifled for his phone. Shame and discomfiture gripped him.

'Yes, I'm here. I'll be a while, Willis.' Discarding his mobile again, he checked the illuminated dial on his watch. It was after four on Saturday morning. His teeth gritted as he attempted to come up with a viable plan that would enable him to smuggle an admittedly very small redhead past the security guards down in the foyer. Otherwise, Poppy's reputation was likely to be in tatters by Monday.

Santino swore under his breath. How much alcohol had he consumed yesterday? There had been the pre-dinner drinks with the Delsens, the wine over the meal he had barely touched and then several brandies in succession. That kind of boozing was not a habit of his. All right, he had not been drunk, but he had not been quite sober either. Alcohol had certainly released all inhibitions and slaughtered his ethics, he conceded grimly.

He looked at Poppy again. Her gorgeous hair was a wild tumble spilling across the leather, one pale bare shoulder and his jacket. She looked adorable, totally at peace and innocent. Only, as he now had very good cause to know, she was no longer *quite* the innocent she had been *before* he laid his womanising hands on her. In the midst of examining his conscience, Santino was appalled to register a powerful temptation just to grab her back into his arms again and kiss her awake. Drink was supposed to be death to the average male libido. *Dio mio*, so much for that old chestnut!

Raking angry hands through his tousled black hair, Santino suppressed a groan. He was furious with himself. How could he have taken advantage of Poppy like that? He struggled to work out how it had happened. They had almost had an argument. He had thrown that vicious comment. She had been leaving when he'd apologised. At that instant, it had somehow seemed unbelievably important to him that she did *not* walk out through that door. Then she had said that about her mother not answering her letters and…?

Ebony brows pleated, Santino gave up on that confusing angle to concentrate on the logical facts that he was more comfortable with. She *worked* for him. Affairs between staff were officially frowned on in Aragone Systems. And guess which smartass had laid down that ground rule for the greater good of interpersonal office relationships and morale? He grimaced. She had been a virgin. He hadn't taken a single precaution. It dawned on him that the last time he had been on a sofa with a woman he might only have been a teenager, but he had exercised a lot more caution then than he had demonstrated the night before. He had screwed up, royally screwed up. In the midst of that lowering acknowledgement, which sat not at all well with his pride, he wondered whether there were still any valentine cards for sale. Finding himself wondering something so inane and out of character unsettled him even more. He breathed in very deep.

Poppy wakened to the sound of a shower running somewhere and her sleepy eyes opened only to widen in dismay when the first thing she saw was her dress lying in a heap on the carpet. A split second later, she realised that she was actually lying under…Santino's jacket! Her heart skipped a beat as she finally appreciated that she had spent most of the night in his office. In *his* arms. As the events that had led up to that staggering development unreeled in her blitzed brain like a very shocking film, she leapt off the sofa like a scalded cat. Praying that Santino would stay in the shower next door long enough for her to make an escape, she dressed at excessive speed.

Tiptoeing to the door, her shoes gripped in one trembling hand, she crept out and then raced for the lift. How could she have behaved like that with Santino? She hadn't even been out on a date with him! Sick with shame and embarrassment, she emerged from the lift and slunk out past the two men chatting at the security desk and mercifully behaving as if she were invisible. The buzzer went, though, to unlock the door and let her out, and her face was as red as a beetroot by the time she reached the street.

'She's a right little looker,' Santino's chauffeur remarked to Willis, the head security guard. A long night of playing poker together had formed an easy camaraderie between the two older men.

'She's a nice friendly kid. That's the first time she's walked out of here without saying goodnight,' Willis said. 'I suppose I can recall the rest of my team now—'

'They'll be getting suspicious if you don't. I'd better get out to the limo and look like I've been dozing. Still, at least you got them shifted before the cleaners come on. Like I said, the boss doesn't usually carry on like this.'

Minutes later, Santino strode from the lift out of breath, black hair still wet from the shower, stormy golden eyes sweeping the foyer in search of Poppy. He couldn't believe she had walked out on him without a word. As if he were some sleazebag of a one-night stand she didn't want to face in daylight! He was outraged. That kind of treatment had never come his way before. Indeed, the clinging habits of certain previous lovers had driven him near to distraction. He had never had one who'd evaporated like scotch mist the first chance she'd got.

He had had hardly any sleep...he was going home, he was going to bed and he'd call on her in the afternoon, he decided. She'd be glad to see him then. She'd appreciate him by then. He hoped she spent the whole lousy morning miserable because that was what she deserved and, in that self-righteous and ripping mood, Santino strode out of the building.

Late that afternoon, Poppy sat on the train watching the countryside fly by with eyes that were blank and faraway. In her mind all she could truly see was a lean, dark, handsome face.

It was amazing how little time it had taken to pack up her belongings and give notice on her bedsit. Everything she possessed fitted into two suitcases. But then she never had been one for gathering clutter, and money to spend on non-essential items had always been in short supply. A fresh start was the best thing, she reminded herself painfully. She could not go back to work at Aragone Systems again. Yes, she could have steeled herself to live down the gossip about that stupid card and her own silliness, but *no*, she could not put herself through the agony of seeing Santino again. She imagined he would be relieved when word of her letter of resignation finally filtered through to him.

Well, she had surely taught herself one good, hard lesson about what happened when a woman flung herself at a man. After all, wasn't that exactly what she had done? Humiliation and guilt engulfed her, for she blamed herself entirely: that childish card telling him that she loved him.

Once Santino had known who the sender was, he wouldn't have been human if that hadn't made him curious. Craig's malice, Santino's concern and her own distress had led to a physical intimacy that would never have developed in normal circumstances. There they had been all alone in the enervating quiet of his office. No doubt even the admiring way she had looked at him had been a provocative encouragement and invitation on male terms. And she might not have much experience with men but every magazine she read warned her that, while nature had programmed women to seek a relationship, men were programmed to seek something an awful lot more basic.

While the train was speeding Poppy towards Wales where her father's aunt, Tilly, lived, Santino was having a very trying dialogue with one of Poppy's former neighbours.

'Nah…haven't seen her for weeks,' the guy with an obvious heavy hangover groused, yawning in Santino's face. 'Maybe she's in there and just doesn't want to answer the door. I had a woman who did that to me. Do you mind if I go back to bed now?'

'Not in the slightest,' Santino breathed grittily.

Santino was now in what was totally unknown territory for him. Maybe Poppy didn't want anything further to do with him. Maybe she *was* in her bedsit not answering the door and praying that he would take the hint and leave her alone. It wasn't exactly a mature response, but a woman who had retained her virtue to the age of twenty-one might well hate his guts for having slept with her when she'd been in such a vulnerable state. If she was so keen to avoid him, and her flight from his office had already brought that message home once, did he have the right to crowd her? Or was he more likely to make a difficult situation worse by pushing too hard too soon? At the end of that logical internal discussion with himself, Santino was still fighting an almost irresistible urge just to smash the door down!

Three weeks later, Poppy was shouting at Tilly's pet geese for lurking behind a gate in an effort to spring a surprise attack on the postman. But the older man was even wilier than the web-footed watchdogs and he leapt into his van unscathed, honked the horn in cheerful one-upmanship and drove off.

Poppy went back into her great-aunt's cottage, clutching the post and the newspaper. Tilly, a small, spry woman with short grey curly hair, well into her seventies but very fit and able, set her book down in favour of the paper.

'Have you got some answers to that ad you placed?' Tilly asked.

'By the looks of it, several,' Poppy answered with determined cheer. 'With a little luck, you'll be shot of your uninvited house guest within a few weeks!'

'You know I *love* having you here,' Tilly scolded.

But her great-aunt's cottage was tiny, perfect for one, crowded for two. Furthermore, Tilly Edwards was one of those rare individuals who actually enjoyed her own company. She had her beloved books and her own set little routine and Poppy did not want to encroach for too long on her hospitality. Within days of her arrival at Tilly's rather isolated home, she had placed an advertisement in a popular magazine seeking employment again as a nanny.

She would take anything—short-term, long-term, whatever came up. The sooner she was working again and too busy to sit feeling sorry for herself, the happier she would be. In the minuscule kitchen, she made a pot of tea for herself and coffee for Tilly. Of recent, she herself had gone off coffee. But then she had pretty much gone off food, too, she conceded wryly, thinking of the irritating bouts of queasiness she had suffered in recent days. Obviously a broken heart led not just to sleepless nights, but poor appetite and indigestion as well. So out of misery might come skinniness. She couldn't even smile at the idea.

She was grateful that she had had enough pride and sense to leave Aragone Systems, but the pain of that sudden severance from all that was familiar and the knowledge that she would never see Santino again was unimaginable and far worse than she had expected. But then it was short, sharp shock treatment, exactly what she had deserved and most needed, she told herself.

'Poppy...' Tilly said from the sitting room.

Poppy moved a few feet back to the doorway. Her great-aunt held up her newspaper. 'Isn't that the man you used to work for?'

Poppy focused on the small black and white photo. Initially the only face she saw was Santino's and then right beside him, beaming like a megawatt light bulb she recognised Jenna Delsen. 'What about him?' she prompted as evenly as she could manage, for one glance even from a distance at Santino in newsprint upset her.

'Seems he's got engaged...an attractive woman, isn't she? Would you like to read it for yourself?' Tilly immediately extended the paper.

'No, thanks. I'll take a look at it later.' Poppy retreated back into the kitchen again and knew that the glimpse she had already had of that damning photo was more than sufficient. She felt incredibly dizzy and assumed that that was the effect of shock. Bracing unsteady hands on the sink unit, she snatched in a stricken breath and shut her anguished eyes tight. *Engaged?* To Jenna Delsen only weeks after he had referred to the beautiful blonde as 'just an old friend'?

Later she went out for a long walk. The strain of trying to behave normally around Tilly had been immense. So, the man you love isn't perfect, after all, she told herself heavily. Shouldn't that make it much easier to get over him? His engagement put a very different complexion on their night together. Santino had *lied* to her. He had lied without hesitation.

He was a two-timing louse, who had simply used her for a casual sexual encounter. Clearly he had already been involved in a relationship with Jenna Delsen that went way beyond the boundaries of platonic friendship.

Three days later, Santino arrived in Wales. Finding out where Poppy's only relative lived had been a long and stony road, which had entailed ditching quite a lot of cool and calling Australia several times before eventually contriving to talk to Poppy's sister-in-law, the doctor. And if Karrie Bishop ever got tired of medicine, secret police forces everywhere would vie for her services. Santino had not appreciated the interrogation he had received, and even less did he appreciate getting lost three times in succession in his efforts to find a remote cottage that he had even begun suspecting Dr Bishop might have only dreamt up out of a desire to punish him!

But there the cottage was, a minute building hiding behind an overgrown hedge, the sort of home loved by those who loathed unexpected visitors, Santino reflected with gritty black humour. His tension was at an all-time high now that he had arrived and he had to think about what he was going to say to Poppy. Oddly enough, Santino had not considered that contentious issue prior to his actual arrival. *Finding* Poppy had been his objective. What he might do with her when he found her was not a problem for his imagination in any way, but what he could reasonably say was something more of a challenge. He missed her at the office? He couldn't get that night out of his mind?

Very unsettled by that absence of cutting-edge inspiration, but too impatient to waste time reflecting on it, Santino climbed out of his sleek car in the teeming rain. When a pair of manic honking geese surged out of nowhere in vicious attack, Santino could happily have wrung their long, scrawny necks, built a bonfire on the spot and cooked them for dinner. The confident conviction that the cottage might lie round every next corner had prevented him from stopping off for lunch and he was in a very aggressive mood.

Hearing the noisy clamour of the geese announcing a rare visitor, Poppy hurried to the front door to yank it open. The car was a startling vivid splash of scarlet against the winter-bare garden. But it was Santino, sleek and immaculate in a charcoal-grey business suit, who knocked most of the air in her lungs clean out of her body.

In the act of holding his feathered opponents at bay with his car door, Santino caught sight of Poppy lurking in the doorway and stilled. The pink sweater made her look cuddly and the floral skirt with the pattern that made him blink was *cheering* on a dull day, he decided, rain dripping down his bronzed features. He just wanted to drag her into the car and drive off with her.

Shock having made Poppy momentarily impervious to his battle with the geese, she stared back at Santino, only dimly wondering why he was standing in heavy rain and getting drenched. What on earth was he doing in Wales? How could he possibly have found out where she was? She met his beautiful eyes, dark as ebony and shameless in their steady appraisal, and she knew she ought to slam the door closed in his face. Seeing him in the flesh again hurt. It only served to refresh painful memories of how much that one night, which had meant so little to him, had meant to her. For just a few hours she had been happier than she had ever hoped to be, but her happiness had flourished in a silly dream world, not in reality, and punishment had not been long in coming.

'Are you planning to call the geese off?' Santino enquired gently. 'Or is this supposed to be a test that picks out the men from the boys?'

Forcing herself free of her nervous paralysis, Poppy lifted the broom by the door and shooed the geese back to allow Santino a free passage indoors.

'*Grazie, cara,*' Santino drawled, smooth as silk.

Her soft mouth wobbled. With an inner quiver, she recalled the liquid flow of Italian words she hadn't understood in the hot, dark pleasure of that night. She turned her burning face away, but not before he had seen the shuttered look in her once trusting and open gaze. She was ashamed of her own weakness. She knew she ought to tell him to go away, but she just didn't have the strength to do that and then never know why he had called in the first place. At least Tilly was out, she thought guiltily, and she wouldn't find herself having to make awkward explanations for his visit.

As Poppy led him into the sitting room Santino bent his dark glossy head to avoid colliding with the low lintel. The room was packed to the gills with furniture and so short of floor space he was reluctant to move in case he knocked something over.

She could not look away from him. Her entire attention was welded to every hard, masculine angle of his bold profile, noting the tension etched there but secretly revelling in the bittersweet pleasure of seeing him again. He turned with measured care to look at her, curling black lashes screening his keen gaze to a sliver of bright, glittering gold.

The atmosphere hummed with undercurrents. Her restive hands clenched together, longing leaping through her in a wildfire wicked surge. Lips parted and moist, in a stillness broken only by the crackling of the fire in the brass grate, she gazed back at him and leant almost imperceptibly forward. Santino needed no further encouragement. Body language like that his male instincts read for him. Without a second of hesitation, he reached for her. Tugging her slight body to him, he meshed one possessive hand into a coil of her Titian red curls and tasted her lush mouth with a slow, smouldering heat that demanded her response.

She was in shaken turmoil at that sensual assault, and a muffled gasp escaped Poppy. His tongue delved with explicit hunger into the tender interior of her mouth. The liquid fire of need ignited in her quivering body faster than the speed of light. She was imprisoned in intimate, rousing contact with his big, powerful length, and her spread fingers travelled from his shoulder up into his luxuriant black hair to hold him to her.

And Santino? In the course of that single kiss, Santino went from wary defensiveness to the very zenith of blazing confidence that he was welcome. Indeed, he was totally convinced that everything was one hundred and one per cent fine. He would have her back in London by midnight. Mission accomplished. Simple, straightforward—why had he ever imagined otherwise?

Then, without the smallest warning, Poppy brought her hands down hard on his arms to break his hold. She wrenched herself free of him with angry tears of self-loathing brimming in her eyes. A wave of dizziness assailed her and she had to push her hands down on the dining table to steady herself and breathe in slow and deep. There was just no excuse for her having let him kiss her when he belonged to another woman. As for him, he was even more of a rat than she had believed he was. He was a hopeless womaniser!

'What's wrong?' Santino breathed in a tone of audible mystification and indeed annoyance.

Her back turned to him, Poppy finally managed to swallow the tears clogging up her vocal cords and she stared with wooden fixity out the window at his car. 'What are you doing in Wales?'

'I had a business meeting in Cardiff earlier.' Santino had decided to play it cool. He was a step ahead of her, he believed and he was already thinking of how to present his having phoned Australia as the ultimate in casual gestures.

But Poppy took the wind right out of his sails by saying, 'I suppose my landlady gave you my forwarding address.'

Infuriatingly, so simple a means of establishing her whereabouts had not even occurred to Santino, but, ignoring that angle, he cut to the chase. 'I wanted to see you.'

He had some nerve. Did he really believe that she was still that naive? In the area on business and at a loose end on a Friday afternoon, he had decided to look her up. Why? Well, she had been free with her favours before and why shouldn't he assume that she would be again? No man could think much of a woman who let him make love to her on his office sofa for a cheap, easy thrill. Poppy felt horribly humiliated.

'I would've thought that most men in these circumstances would've been glad *not* to see me again,' Poppy countered painfully in a small voice.

Santino wondered why it was that, when she had run to the other side of the country to avoid *him*, he was being accused of not wanting to see *her*. Suddenly he too was asking himself what he was doing in Wales. Suddenly he suspected that he could well be within an ace of making a total ass of himself.

'Why would you assume that?' Santino enquired.

'Well, if you don't know that for yourself, I'm certainly not going to be the one to remind you!' Poppy condemned chokily, for she refused to lower herself to the level of mentioning Jenna Delsen's name. She refused to give him that much satisfaction. No doubt his ego would relish the belief that she was heartbroken at the news of his engagement. Or maybe he imagined that she was still in blissful ignorance of the true nature of his relationship with the beautiful blonde.

Unable to work out exactly where the unproductive dialogue was going, Santino decided that it was time to be blunt. 'Why did you send me a card telling me that you loved me?'

If the window had been open at that moment, Poppy would have scrambled through it and fled without hesitation. Aghast at that loaded question, she went rigid.

'I don't think that's an unreasonable question,' Santino continued, tension flattening his accented drawl into the command tone he used at work. 'And I'm tired of talking to your back.'

Seething discomfiture flamed hot colour into Poppy's cheeks, but pride came to her rescue. Flipping round on taut legs, she encountered brilliant dark-as-midnight eyes and forced a dismissive shrug. 'For goodness sake...the valentine card was a joke!'

The silence that fell seemed to last for ever.

Santino had gone very still, his strong bone structure clenching hard. 'A joke...?' A flame of raw derision flared in his gaze as he absorbed that demeaning explanation. The most obvious explanation, yet one that for some reason he had never considered. 'What are you...fourteen years old or something?'

'Or something...' Her nails were digging purple welts into her damp palms while she struggled to control the wobble that had developed in her knee joints. 'It was just a stupid joke...and then Craig got hold of it and blew it up into something else and I ended up looking like an idiot!'

'I hope you don't also end up pregnant,' Santino framed with a ragged edge to his dark, deep drawl, wide, sensual mouth compressed, the pallor of anger lightening the bronzed skin round his hard jawline. 'I doubt very much that that would strike even you as a joke.'

Poppy gazed back at him in appalled silence, her tongue cleaving to the roof of her mouth, for not once since that night had she even considered that there might be consequences. She had, without ever really thinking about it, simply assumed that he had taken care of that risk for her.

'You mean, you *didn't*…?' she began shakily.

'I'm afraid not.' Brooding dark eyes acknowledging the level of her dismay and disconcertion, Santino released his breath in a slow speaking hiss of regret. 'But I do accept that, whatever happens, the responsibility is mine.'

CHAPTER SIX

AT THAT moment, Poppy wanted to curl up in a ball like a toddler and cry her heart out, for what Santino had just revealed shed a very different light on what had motivated his visit.

Since when had she got so vain that she believed Santino Aragone was so bereft of females willing to share his bed that he had sought her out in Wales? The idea was laughable, *ridiculous*! Now she was remembering his tension when he'd first arrived. Had she precipitated that kiss? Had that been her fault once again? Or just one of those crazy mishaps that occurred when people were all wound up and not really knowing how to react or what to say?

Well, it scarcely mattered now, Poppy conceded painfully. Santino had come to find her and speak to her for a very good reason, and indeed the fact that he had made the effort told her much more about his strength of character than anything else. He had been worried that he might have got her pregnant. That was the only reason he had taken the trouble to seek her out again. Most men, particularly one who had just asked or had been about to ask another woman to marry him, would have done nothing and just hoped for the best. But Santino had *not* taken the easy way out.

'The night of the party...' Santino caught and held her swift upward glance '...we had both been drinking. I have never been so reckless, but then I don't have a history of that kind of behaviour and I know that you had no history at all.'

Feverish colour flared in Poppy's tense face. She was still in shock at her own naivety, her own foolish, pitiful assumptions about why he had come to see her. It took enormous will-power for her to confront the more serious issue. Might she have conceived that night? A belated rethink on what might have caused her recent bouts of nauseous disinterest in food froze Poppy to the spot. And what about the little dizzy turns she had written off as being the results of not eating or sleeping well? *Was* it possible that she was pregnant? She had never bothered to keep track of her own cycle. How long had it been since the party? A couple of weeks, *more*? Her brain was in turmoil, refusing to function. When had she last…? She couldn't remember. It seemed like a long time ago. Santino had just delivered what had to be the ultimate male put-down. He had come to tell *her* she might be pregnant!

Poppy shifted her head in a dazed motion. 'I really don't know yet if I'm…you know…I don't know…er…either way.'

Santino took a slight step forward. She looked so much like a terrified teenager. She couldn't even find the words to talk about conception. He wanted to close his arms round her, drive out the panic and uncertainty clouding her eyes, tell her that she had nothing to worry about and that he would look after her. And then he stiffened, sudden bitter anger flaring through him, making him suppress his own natural instincts. The valentine card had been a joke, a childish, stupid joke with no sense that he could see, but then someone might have dared her to do it for a laugh. How did he know? He didn't feel as if he knew anything any more about Poppy.

In fact, the more Santino thought of how she had behaved, the more alienated he felt. She wasn't in love with him, never had been in love with him. Even a little dose of infatuation would have lasted longer than a couple of weeks. Maybe she had slept with him because she had decided it was time she acquired some experience. Whatever, her behaviour ever since had spoken for her: she didn't want to see him and preferred to forget about that night. In fact, she could not have made her feelings clearer. She had jacked in her job, left London. Exactly why had he gone to such extraordinary lengths to locate her? Had he become such an arrogant jerk that he couldn't accept a woman's rejection?

'Presumably you'll know whether or not you're pregnant very soon,' Santino drawled without any expression at all. 'If you are, please get in touch with me immediately and we'll deal with it together. Obviously I will give you my support. You know how to reach me.'

His beautiful dark eyes were still level but his detachment was noticeable and complete. Poppy could feel that change like a wall he had thrown up between them. He wanted to leave. She could feel that, too. But then why not? It hadn't been a very pleasant visit for him to have to make, she recognised miserably. It had been a waste of time too when she had been unable to tell him that he had nothing to worry about. Naturally he would be praying that there would be no repercussions from that night and that awareness prevented her from sharing her own misgivings. Why say anything when she might well be fretting about nothing?

Santino strode towards his car and then swung back for one last look at her. 'Look after yourself,' he offered gruffly.

Feeling as if she were dying inside, Poppy stood like a statue watching the car reverse out. She had the most terrible urge to run after it and tell him that, even though she ought to hate him, she still loved him. But what would he want to know that for? He *had* to be in love with Jenna.

A couple of miles down the road, Santino brought the car to a halt, buzzed down the window and drank in a great lungful of the fresh, rain-wet air. *Mission accomplished?* A raw-edged laugh, empty of all humour, broke from him. Why was he chickening out of confronting the obvious: his success scores before the sofa, and on the sofa, had been nil. Everything that had struck him as fantastic and very special had left her distinctly underwhelmed. She hadn't even offered him a cup of coffee. All the way to Wales for the privilege of being shot down in flames in the space of ten minutes!

Thinking of the stupid, naff valentine card he had bought for her, a violent miasma of emotion lanced through Santino. He just wanted to smash something. He didn't want to think about her. In fact he was determined not to think about her. Of course, she wasn't going to be pregnant! Off the top of his head, he could have named three young, healthy married couples tying themselves in knots in a desperate effort to conceive a child. The chances of his having fathered a baby in one night were slim and surely she would have known by now? He would check into a hotel, get something to eat…only he wasn't hungry any more.

So he would check into a hotel and have a lost weekend. Why? He just felt like it! He wanted to drink himself into a stupor. He was off women, really, really *seriously* off women.

Three days later, Poppy learned that she was indeed pregnant.

During the weekend, she had had to content herself with purchasing a pregnancy test kit. When the test had come up positive, she'd barely slept for the following two nights. Unsure of how reliable a home test was, she'd made an appointment at her local surgery. When the doctor gave her the same confirmation and discussed options with her, she already knew that she didn't want a termination. She loved children, had always hoped that some day she would have some of her own, but that prospect had until then existed in some dim, distant future. Now that a baby, Santino's baby, was a much more immediate reality, she also knew she had some hard thinking to do about how she intended to manage.

At first, she believed that she could steel herself to phone Santino to tell him that she was carrying his child, but when it came to the point she couldn't face it. Santino was engaged to Jenna. Like it or not, what she had to tell him was very bad news on his terms. She had her pride too and she didn't want to risk getting all weepy and apologetic on the phone, did she? As she wasn't prepared to consider a termination, she decided that it would be less painful all round if she wrote a letter spelling out her intentions.

So, Poppy sat in Tilly's narrow little guest-room bed and tried to write a letter. But she kept on sitting there and trying to write it and failing and scrunching up her every attempt and ended up in floods of miserable tears.

Finally, she stopped trying to save face and just let her own honest feelings speak for her in what she wrote. After all, did she really want Santino to go on thinking now that the valentine card had just been a cheap, silly joke? That their baby had been conceived as a result of such a joke? Poppy cringed at that image. Some day, she would want to tell their child that she had loved his father and that truth was surely more important than her own pride.

When it dawned on Poppy that she would have to send the letter to Aragone Systems because she *still* didn't know Santino's home address and he wasn't in the phone book either, she was careful to print 'Private and Confidential' in block capitals on one corner of the envelope. Once it was in the post, she tried not to think about it. The ball was in his court now. She would just have to wait and see what happened.

During the following week she was offered interviews with two families in search of a nanny, in fact *desperate* for a nanny. Qualified nannies, it seemed, were in even shorter supply than they had been when she had first emerged from her training. But did she admit she was pregnant or not? She decided that she would be happier being honest from the outset as she would need time off to attend pre-natal hospital appointments, and then of course she would have a baby in tow. At the same time, on every occasion that Tilly's phone rang, her heart would start banging like a drum and she would think that it was Santino calling her. But Santino *didn't* call and watching the post proved to be no more productive.

But then, had she but known it, Santino never received her letter. He was in Italy when it arrived and Craig Belston was working his last day at Aragone Systems. An astute operator, Craig had recognised that his promotion prospects were slim if he stayed; Santino had been cold with him ever since the night of that party. Although Craig had found lucrative employment elsewhere, his resentment at what a little teasing of Poppy Bishop had cost him still rankled. He examined the letter, his mouth twisting at the 'P. Bishop' and return address printed on the back of the envelope. Walking over to the tall drinks cabinet, which had of recent contained nothing stronger than soft drinks and mineral water, he dropped the letter down between it and the wall and he smiled.

Within a month Poppy had left Wales and started work as a nanny again. Initially shocked that Santino had not responded to her letter, she grew more cynical as time passed. After all, his silence was in itself an answer, wasn't it? Confronted with the worst-case scenario, Santino had decided that he didn't want to know about the baby. Why had she swallowed all that impressive guff about him being willing to take responsibility? Why once again had she begun thinking of him as an essentially decent guy?

After all, Santino had lied that night about Jenna to get her onto that sofa, so, why shouldn't he have lied again? She was on her own in *every* way and, for the sake of the child she was expecting, she reckoned that she had better get used to the idea.

CHAPTER SEVEN

'YES, that uniform looks the thing, all right. Turn round,' Daphne Brewett urged Poppy, her be-ringed hands clasped together, an approving smile blooming on her plump, attractive face. 'You look like a *proper* nanny now, luv. No chance of folk mistaking you for one of those au pair girls, who work for pocket change! What do you think, Harold?'

Her balding husband, Harold, removed his admiring gaze with reluctance from Poppy's slim black nylon-clad ankles. 'Does anyone but the Royals put their nannies in uniform these days?' he enquired in his refined public school accent, his tone apologetic.

Daphne stuck her hands on her ample hips and skewered him with one warning glance. 'Poppy's wearing a uniform...OK?' she rapped out loudly.

Harold nodded in submission and picked up his newspaper. Poppy, who had been toying with the idea of mentioning that she was afraid that the fussy white apron and the frilly little hat were *definitely* over the top, thought better of it. Daphne had a terrible temper and Harold might be a very astute and respected business tycoon, but he was terrified of his wife and knew when to keep quiet. Poppy reminded herself that she was earning an enormous salary. If pleasing Daphne meant dressing like a cross between a French maid and a Victorian nurse, she would just have to put up with it. After all, Daphne had been broad-minded enough to hire a nanny who came with a very young child of her own in tow. Indeed, Daphne had been warmly accepting of what had struck other potential employers as a serious drawback.

'Right...' Having vanquished Harold, Daphne turned her attention on Poppy again. 'You have the kiddies packed and ready for two this afternoon. We're off to Torrisbrooke Priory for the weekend. That'll be a treat for you. You can look forward to seeing some real landed gentry there,' she said with unhidden satisfaction.

Poppy walked out of the drawing room. Three children were seated on the stairs: Tristram, aged ten, Emily Jane, aged eight, Rollo, aged five, all blond and blue-eyed and very unspoilt and pleasant children. Daphne Brewett might be a very domineering personality but beggars could not be choosers, Poppy reminded herself squarely, determined to make the best of her recent employment with the family.

'Well, did you tell Ma how dumb you looked?' Tris asked with rich cynicism.

Poppy shook her head in wincing apology.

'I'm not going to be seen dead with you in that daft get-up!' Tris warned her.

'It's very uncool,' Emily Jane pronounced in a pained tone.

'You look funny!' Rollo giggled. 'I like your silly hat.'

With a rueful grin, Poppy went over to the pram parked below the stairs. Florenza was wide awake, big blue eyes sparkling beneath her soft mop of tiny black curls. Poppy reached in and scooped her daughter out to take her back upstairs again. Florenza was three months old, cute as a button, and the undeniable centre of her adoring mother's world.

'Who lives at Torisbrooke Priory?' Poppy asked Tris on the way upstairs.

'Dunno. But Ma thinks the invitation's really great, so it's probably somebody posh with a title. I wish she'd just leave us at home,' he grumbled. 'She's really embarrassing in other people's houses.'

'Don't talk about your mother like that,' Poppy reproved.

'I don't like people laughing at her,' Tris said defensively.

Ignoring that, for to deny that Daphne could be both vulgar and comical in her desire to impress all with the conspicuous extent of the Brewett wealth, was impossible.

At four that afternoon, the Brewett cavalcade of limousines drove at a stately pace up the long, wooded, winding drive to Torrisbrooke Priory. A vast and ancient building appeared round the final bend. It was built of weathered Tudor brick, winter sunshine glittering over the many mullioned windows, and

Poppy gazed out at it with interest. Half a dozen big cars were already parked on the gravel frontage.

A venerable butler stood at the gothic arched front door in readiness. Daphne and Harold descended from the first limo. Florenza clasped in her arms and wearing the gabardine raincoat that went with her uniform, Poppy climbed out of the second limo in the wake of the children. The third limo was just for the luggage: Daphne did not travel light.

When a very tall, dark male strolled down the steps to greet her employers, Poppy's steps faltered. It couldn't be, it couldn't possibly be! But as her shattered eyes focused on the lean, devastatingly handsome dark features that still haunted her dreams on a shamefully regular basis, she saw that it truly was...it *was* Santino Aragone! Sheer, disbelieving panic afflicted her. Was he their host? Why else would he be shaking hands with Harold? Did that mean that the priory belonged to Santino?

Daphne summoned her children to her side to introduce them. In the background, Poppy hovered. There was no place to go, no place to hide. At the exact moment that Santino registered her presence, Poppy froze, heart thumping so hard she felt sick, her taut face pale as milk. His brilliant dark eyes welded to her and just stayed there, his surprise unconcealed.

'And this is our nanny, Poppy,' Daphne trilled in full swing. 'And little Flo.'

Her blue eyes achingly vulnerable, Poppy's chin nonetheless came up in a sudden defiant tilt. What did she have to be embarrassed about? Santino was the one who ought to be embarrassed! She noted that as his piercing gaze suddenly veiled, he did not succumb to the temptation of stealing so much as a glance at his own daughter.

'Poppy and I have met before. She used to work in Aragone Systems,' Santino remarked without any apparent discomfiture. 'Let's go inside. It's cold.'

While Daphne chattered cheerfully about what a small world it was, Santino was in shock but refusing to acknowledge it. A coincidence and life was full of them, he told himself. Poppy was the Brewetts' nanny and she would be busy with their children all weekend. It was almost a year to the day *since*... No,

no way was he revisiting that memory lane. A baby wailed. As
Santino hadn't noticed a baby in the party, he turned his head
in bewilderment, following the sound right back to source: the
small bundle cradled in Poppy's arms.

'I didn't realise you had a new baby,' he said to Daphne,
struggling to act the part of interested host, endeavouring to force
a relaxed smile to his taut features.

'Oh, the baby's not ours.' Daphne loosed a girlish giggle,
flattered by Santino's misapprehension because she was pushing
fifty. 'Three was quite enough for me! Flo is Poppy's kiddy.'

At the foot of the glorious oak carved staircase where the
butler was waiting to show her upstairs, Poppy stared at Santino
with very wide blue eyes. What on earth was he playing at?
When his startled gaze zeroed in on her with sudden questioning
force, she was at a complete loss. Why was he acting so surprised? Hadn't he appreciated that pregnancies most often led to
births and little babies?

'Her name's Florenza,' Tris piped up. 'Flo's just what Ma
calls her.'

'Florenza…' Santino repeated, ebony brows pleating.

'It's I-talian,' Daphne told him helpfully.

Santino angled a charged scrutiny at the little squirming bundle. He was suffering from information overload. Was Florenza
his child? What age was the little girl? She was wrapped in a
shawl and, the way she was being held, the shawl was all he
could see. She might be a newborn baby, she might be some
other man's child. She *couldn't* be his daughter! Poppy would
have told him, wouldn't she?

Fabulous cheekbones prominent below his bronzed skin,
Santino dredged his attention from the mystery bundle, encountered a speculative look from Daphne Brewett's keen gaze and
hastened to show his guests into the drawing room.

Poppy climbed the stairs in a daze, beneath which a growing
turmoil of emotions seethed. Santino had been astounded when
Daphne had informed him that the baby was her nanny's. He
had stared at Florenza much as though she were a Pandora's
box ready to fly open and cause a storm of catastrophe. A tremor
ran through Poppy and her arms tightened round her tiny daugh-

ter. Why was she shrinking from facing the obvious explanation for Santino's incredulity? Evidently, Santino had assumed that without his support she would *not* continue her pregnancy. Well, how else could she interpret his shocked reaction to Florenza's existence?

Was Jenna waiting in that drawing room downstairs? Jenna in her gracious role of hostess as Santino's wife? Had they got married during the last year? At that awful thought, a cold, clammy chill slid down Poppy's spine and her sensitive tummy clenched in protest. For the first time, she regretted not having allowed herself to check out whether or not that wedding had taken place as yet. But refusing to allow herself to seek any information whatsoever about Santino Aragone's life had been a necessary defence mechanism. She had brought down a curtain on the past and disciplined herself to live only in the present.

'Is this Mr Aragone's home?' she enquired of the elderly butler, Jenkins, whose steps were slowing with each step up the stairs.

'Yes, madam,' he wheezed and, as he was so clearly in no fit state to answer any further questions, Poppy had to content herself with that.

Three hours later, having supervised a late and riotous tea with the children that had been served in a small dining room on the ground floor, Poppy set up Florenza's bright and cosy travel cot in the nursery and tucked her up for the night. Poppy was tired. Her days started at six when Florenza wakened and she was grateful that it was her night off. Although impressing that necessity on Daphne had been a challenge, she conceded ruefully. But she was painfully aware that live-in nannies had to define boundaries or she would soon find herself on call twenty-four hours a day.

The priory was a simply huge house. Poppy reflected that she might well contrive to stay the weekend without seeing Santino again. Unhappily, she was conscious of a dangerous craving to nonetheless throw herself in his path for a showdown. He *deserved* to be told what a rat he was! Removing her elaborate uniform with a grimace of relief, she ran a bath for herself in the bathroom beside the nursery and got in to have a soak.

In the library downstairs, undercover of having announced the necessity of making an urgent call, Santino was delving in frustration through a very old book on babies. All he needed to know was what weight the average baby was when it was born. Armed with that knowledge, he might then take a subtle peek at Poppy's baby and work out whether it was within the realms of possibility that Florenza was *his* baby, too. Why not just ask Poppy? That would entail a serious loss of face that Santino was unwilling to consider.

Convinced that Poppy would be down in the basement swimming pool supervising the Brewett children, Santino strolled into the nursery on the top floor. The grand Edwardian cot was unoccupied but the lurid plastic and mesh contraption set beside it contained his quarry. Breathing in deep, Santino advanced as quietly as he could to steal a glance over the padded rim. The first thing he saw was a downy fluff of black curls and then a pair of soft blue unblinking eyes focused on him. His first startled thought was that, for a baby, Florenza was remarkably pretty.

But it was hard to say which of them was the most surprised. Santino, who had paid only the most fleeting attention to friends' babies, fully believed that infants only operated on two modes: screeching or sleeping. He had *expected* Florenza to be asleep. Aghast, he watched Florenza's big eyes flash like an intruder-tracking device, her tiny nose screwing up as her little rosebud mouth began to open.

Santino backed off fast. But even though he was bracing himself, the threatened screech never came. Instead, Florenza turned her little head to peer at him through the mesh. When he dared to inch forward again, Florenza's tiny face tensed in warning. It dawned on him that lifting the baby to gauge her weight was not a viable option. She was a really sharp, on-the-ball baby, ready to shriek like a fire alarm at the first sign of a stranger getting too close, and he didn't want to frighten her.

Wrapped in a bath towel and barefoot, Poppy glanced into the nursery just to check on Florenza before she went to get dressed and could not credit what she was seeing. Her lips parted on a demand to know what Santino thought he was doing, but the manner in which her tiny daughter was holding him at bay was actually very funny. However, she only found it funny for about the space of ten seconds. For as she studied Santino's bold, masculine profile and switched her strained gaze to Florenza's matching dark eyes a wealth of powerful emotion overwhelmed Poppy without warning. Father and daughter didn't even know each other and never would in the normal way. Curiosity might have brought Santino to the nursery, but that did not mean he had suffered a sudden sea change in conscience.

As an odd choky little gasp sounded behind him, Santino swung round and caught only the merest glimpse of Poppy's convulsed face as she spun away and raced into the bedroom across the corridor, slamming the door in her wake.

Sobs catching in her throat, she sank down at the foot of the bed and buried her head in her arms. She hated him, she *really* hated him! She was thinking of every bad experience she had had in the months since that night they had shared, not least having been the only woman in the maternity ward without a single visitor. In addition, her parents' initially shocked and censorious reaction to the revelation of a grandchild born out of wedlock had increased Poppy's distress. Although relations had since been smoothed over and gifts had been sent, Poppy remained painfully aware that once again she had disappointed her family.

When the door opened and Santino strode in, Poppy was astonished for she had not expected him to risk forcing a confrontation in his own home. But there he stood, six feet three inches of lean, powerful masculinity, apparently so impervious to remorse that he could face her with his arrogant head high, his stubborn jaw at an angle and without any shade of discomfiture. For a timeless few seconds, she drank her fill of looking at him. He was still absolutely gorgeous, she noted resentfully, and she was ashamed to feel the quickened beat of her own heart, the licking tension of excitement and the taunting curl of heat slivering through her. In despair at her own weakness, she veiled her gaze.

'I only have one question...' Santino breathed in the taut silence. 'Is Florenza mine?'

'Are you out of your mind?' Poppy gasped.

What was he trying to do? Portray her as some loose woman, who might not know the paternity of her own child? How much lower could a guy sink than to insinuate that?

Taut as a high-voltage wire, Santino was endeavouring to make sense of the incomprehensible while resisting what had become a predictable instinct when Poppy was upset: a need to haul her into his arms that was so strong only fierce will power kept him at the other side of the room. He was also working very hard at not allowing his attention to roam one inch below her collar bone, where an expanse of smooth, creamy cleavage took over before vanishing beneath the tightly wrapped towel.

'You know very well that Florenza's yours,' Poppy splintered back at him, her bright tousled head coming up, her blue eyes angry. 'So don't you *dare* ask me a question like that!'

Knocked back by that accusing confirmation that Florenza was his child, momentarily blind to even the allurement of Poppy's exquisite shape in a towel, Santino could not immediately come up with a response. He was a father. He had a daughter. His mother was a grandparent. He was an unmarried father with a baby sleeping in a plastic playpen. His baby's mother hated him *so* much she hadn't even been able to persuade herself to accept his support, financially or in any other way…

Poppy collided with his stunning dark-as-midnight gaze and tensed at the sight of the pain and regret that he couldn't hide. 'You don't even know what to say to me, do you?'

'No…' Santino acknowledged hoarsely, lean hands coiling into fists and uncoiling only slowly again.

'I've turned up like a bad penny in the wrong place.' Poppy said what she assumed he was thinking. 'Is Jenna downstairs?'

'Jenna?' Santino echoed with a frown. 'Jenna who?'

Poppy flew upright and threw the first thing that came to her hand. A shoe thumped Santino in the chest. The second shoe caught him quite a painful clip on the ear. Poppy blazed back at him in a passion that shook him even more, 'Jenna…*who*? Jenna Delsen, your fiancée, whom you described as *just* an old friend when it suited you! You lying louse, Santino Aragone!'

Santino cast aside the second shoe, brilliant eyes narrowed in astonishment. 'I'm not engaged to Jenna. She *is* an old friend and I was a guest at her wedding last summer.'

In wordless incredulity, Poppy stared back at him, but a hollow, sick sensation was already spreading through her trembling body. He had been a guest at Jenna's wedding? Such a statement had a serious ring of truth.

Lean, strong face taut, Santino moved expressive hands in a gesture of bewilderment. 'Where on earth did you get the idea that I had got engaged to Jenna?'

Poppy snatched in a stark, quivering breath. 'It was in a newspaper…a picture of you and Jenna. It said you were engaged…er…but I never looked at it that closely.'

Santino stilled then, black brows drawing together. 'An old friend did phone me to congratulate me on my supposed engagement last year,' he recalled with an obvious effort, his frown deepening. 'The newspaper he mentioned had used an old picture of Jenna and I together and he'd misread the couple of lines below about her engagement party. Her fiancé, David, *was* named but he hadn't picked up on it.'

Silence fell like a smothering blanket of snow.

Poppy was appalled at the explanation that Santino had just proffered. Tilly had only glanced at the item because she had recognised Santino and Tilly only ever skimmed through newspapers. When her great niece had failed to display any interest in the seeming fact that her former employer had got engaged, Tilly would, in all probability, not have bothered to look back at it again. And Poppy had been far too cut up, far too much of a coward, to pick up that newspaper and read exactly what it had said for herself.

'Tell me,' Santino asked very drily, 'exactly when did you see that newspaper and decide that I was an outright liar?'

Her breath snarled up in her throat. It had been too much to hope that he would not immediately put together what she had believed him capable of doing. Squirming with guilty unease and embarrassment and a whole host of other, much more confused emotions, Poppy admitted shakily, 'Before you came to Wales…'

A harsh laugh that was no laugh at all was dredged from

Santino, bitter comprehension stamped in his brooding features as he turned sizzling dark golden eyes back on her in proud and angry challenge. '*Per meraviglia*…you had some opinion of me! You decided I'd been cheating on another woman with you. No wonder you were so surprised to see me in Wales, but you didn't have the decency to face me with your convictions, did you?'

Poppy gulped. 'I—'

'I didn't have a clue what I was walking into that day,' Santino framed in a low-pitched raw undertone, treating her to another searing appraisal that shamed her even more. 'But all the time that I was trying to make sense of your bewildering behaviour, you were thinking I was a two-timing liar with no principles and no conscience!'

'Santino…I'm *sorry*!' Poppy gasped.

His lean powerful face stayed hard and unimpressed. 'You tell our daughter you're sorry. Don't waste your breath on me!'

'No…you tell her you're sorry,' Poppy dared hoarsely. 'You're the one who decided you didn't want anything to do with her.'

'I didn't even know she *existed*!' Santino's temper finally broke free of all restraint. 'How the blazes could I have had anything to do with a child I wasn't aware had even been born?'

'But I wrote to you telling you I was pregnant,' Poppy protested.

'I didn't get a letter and why would you write anyway? Why trust an important and private communication of that nature to the vagaries of the post? Why not just phone?' Santino demanded, immediately dubious of her claim that there had ever been a letter.

Poppy closed her eyes and swallowed hard in an effort to pull herself together. It was obvious that her letter must have gone astray. Only then did she recall once reading that thousands of letters went missing in the mail every year. But why that one desperately important letter? Why *her* letter? She could have wept.

'Look, I have thirty-odd people waiting dinner for me downstairs,' Santino admitted curtly. 'I don't have time to handle this right now.'

'There *was* a letter,' Poppy repeated unsteadily.

Before he shut the door, Santino dealt her a derisive look. 'So what if there was?' he derided, turning the tables on her afresh. 'What kind of a woman lets her child's whole future rest on one miserable letter?'

CHAPTER EIGHT

STRIVING to look as though she had not passed a sleepless night waiting for the phone by her bed to ring or even the sound of a masculine footstep, Poppy knocked on her employer's bedroom door and entered. 'Tris said you wanted to see me.'

Still lying in bed, clad in an elaborate satin bed jacket, Daphne treated her to a rather glum appraisal. 'Yes. It's a shame about that uniform, though. I bet you it won't fit the next nanny.'

Poppy stilled. 'I'm sorry…er…what next nanny?'

With a sigh, Daphne settled rueful eyes on Poppy. 'Santino had a little chat with me last night. Didn't he mention it?'

Her colour rising, Poppy stiffened. 'No.'

'You just can't work for us any more, luv. Once Santino told me that little Flo is his, I saw where he was coming from all right,' Daphne continued with a speaking grimace. 'Naturally he doesn't want you running about fetching and carrying for my kids!'

'Doesn't he, indeed?' Her face burning fierily at Santino's most unexpected lack of discretion, Poppy was scarcely able to credit her own hearing.

'It wouldn't suit us either.' Daphne gave her an apologetic look. 'The point is, Harold and Santino do business together. You're the mother of Santino's kid and you working for us, well, it just wouldn't look or feel right now.'

It was obvious that the older woman had already made up her mind on that score.

'You don't even want me to work my notice?'

'No. Santino's arranged for an agency nanny for what's left of the weekend. He's a decent bloke, Poppy…' Daphne told her bluntly. 'I don't see why you should be angry with him for wanting to do what's right by you and take care of you and that little baby.'

A minute later, Poppy stalked down the corridor and then

down flight after flight of stairs until she was literally giddy with speed and fury. She arrived in a breathless whirl in the main hall. Santino appeared in a doorway. He ran his lethally eloquent dark eyes from the crown of the frilly hat perched at a lopsided angle in her thick, rebellious hair to the starched apron that topped the shadow-striped dress beneath.

'Good morning, Mary Poppins,' he murmured lazily. 'Remind me to buy you more black stockings, but you can ditch the rest of the outfit.'

'Yes, I can, can't I?' Poppy hissed. 'Especially when you've just had me thrown out of my job!'

Striding forward, Santino closed a hand over hers and pressed her into the room he had emerged from. 'We don't need an audience for this dialogue, *cara*.'

'I'm surprised you care! You had no trouble last night baring my deepest secrets to Daphne Brewett!' Poppy condemned.

'Why should Florenza be a secret? I'm proud to be her father and I have no intention of concealing our relationship,' Santino stated with an amount of conviction that shook her. 'And please don't tell me that you're breaking your heart at the prospect of taking off that ludicrous uniform!'

Poppy refused to back down. 'It was a good job, well paid and with considerate employers—'

'Yet the rumour is that the Brewetts still can't keep domestic staff. Do you know why?' Santino enquired sardonically. '*Daphne*. She's wonderfully kind and friendly most of the time. But she can't control her temper and she becomes much more abusive than the average employee is willing to tolerate these days. Haven't you crossed her yet? It doesn't take much to annoy her.'

Poppy paled, reluctant to recall the older woman's worryingly sharp reproof the previous afternoon when she had been five minutes late getting the children downstairs with all their luggage.

'But then you've only been working for them for a few weeks and she'll still be wary, but I do assure you that if you had stayed much longer, you would have felt the rough edge of Daphne's tongue. She's famous for it.'

'Well, I still don't think that that gave you the right to interfere,' Poppy retorted curtly. 'I can look after myself.'

'But unfortunately, you're not the only person involved here. I want what's best for all *three* of us.' Santino surveyed her with level dark golden eyes, willing her to listen to him. 'I don't see the point in a further exchange of recriminations. Life's too short. I also want to share in Florenza's life. For that reason, I'm willing to ask you to marry me...'

Shock held Poppy still, but the way he had framed that statement also lacerated her pride. He was 'willing' to ask her to marry him? Big deal! Her first marriage proposal and he shot it at her when she was seething with angry turmoil at the manner in which he had attempted to take control of her life. Now it seemed that he had taken away her security so that he could offer her another kind of security. That of being a wife. *His wife.* Her lips trembled and she sealed them.

'Possibly I messed up the delivery of that,' Santino conceded as the tense silence stretched to breaking-point. 'I *do* want to marry you.'

Poppy spun away to gaze out the window at the rolling parkland and mature trees that gave the priory such a beautiful setting. Of course, he didn't *want* to marry her! In Daphne's parlance, Santino was offering to do 'the right thing' by her. He had got her pregnant and he saw marriage as the most responsible means of making amends. He was really lucky that she wasn't the sort of female who would snatch at his offer just because he was rich, successful and gorgeous. Or even because she still loved him, she conceded painfully.

Poppy flipped round to meet Santino's intense dark scrutiny, her face tight with strain. 'Our relationship has only been an ongoing catastrophe,' she framed unevenly.

His jawline clenched. 'That's not how I would describe it—'

'When you called on me at Tilly's, you said pretty much the same thing,' Poppy reminded him. 'I ended up on that sofa because you had had too much to drink and you regretted it. That's no basis for a marriage and, anyway, I don't want to be married to some guy who thinks it's his *duty* to put a ring on my finger!'

'Duty doesn't come into this.' Santino groaned in sudden

exasperation. 'We made love because I couldn't keep my distance from you, because I couldn't help myself, *cara*—'

'Yes, but—'

'Just looking at you burns me up. Always did...*still* does,' Santino intoned, striding forward to close his lean hands round hers. 'That's not a catastrophe, that's fierce attraction. If you hadn't worked for me, we would have got together a lot sooner.'

'I can't believe that...' But even so, it was an assurance that Poppy longed to believe.

Santino reached up and whisked the frilly hat from her hair and tossed it aside.

'What are you doing?' she whispered.

The sudden slashing smile that she had feared she might never see again flashed out, lightening his lean, dark features and yanking at every fibre of her resistance. He undid the apron, removed it with careful hands and put it aside, too. Then he unbuttoned the high collar of her dress.

'You want me to prove how much you excite me?' Santino enquired with husky mesmeric intensity, molten golden eyes scanning her with anticipation. 'Ready and willing, *cara mia*.'

A little quiver of sensual response rippled through Poppy's taut frame. 'Don't...'

'Don't what?' Santino asked, flicking back the collar to press his lips to the base of her slender throat, sending such a shock wave of instantaneous response leaping through her that she let her head tip back heavily on her neck, her untouched mouth tingling, literally aching for the hungry heat of his. 'Don't do *this*...?'

He discovered a pulse point just below her ear and lingered there. She trembled, heard herself moan and she grabbed his jacket for support, feeling herself drowning in the melting pleasure she had worked so hard to forget. Then, he framed the feverish flush on her cheekbones with spread fingers and kissed her just once, hard and fast, demanding and urgent, leaving her wanting so much more.

'Now do you believe I really want you?' Santino breathed raggedly.

Poppy stumbled back from him, lips still throbbing and body

still thrumming from that little demonstration against which she had discovered she was without defence. He could turn her into a shameless hussy with incredible ease, but he didn't *love* her. 'It wouldn't work…us, I mean.'

'Why not?'

'Don't you know how to take no for an answer?' Poppy muttered shakily from the door.

'I took it the last time. It gained me a daughter of three months old whom I have still to meet.' As Santino made that raw retaliation Poppy's discomfited gaze slewed from his and she left the room and was relieved when he didn't follow her, for he had given her a lot to think about.

Getting changed into jeans and a sweater, Poppy put Florenza in her buggy and went out for a walk. She was starting to see that all she had ever done with Santino was think the worst of his motivations and run away as fast as her legs could carry her. Twelve months ago, she had still had a lot of growing up left to do. So many misunderstandings might have been avoided had she not performed a vanishing act after the staff party. She had reacted like an embarrassed little girl, afraid to face reality after the fantasy of the night. Scared of getting hurt, she had ended up just as hurt anyway. She had assumed that everything that had happened between them had somehow been *her* fault and had denied them both the chance to explore their feelings.

Poppy sat down on a fallen log below the trees. In the same way she had just accepted that Santino was engaged to Jenna Delsen and had hidden behind her pride rather than confront him. But what she could forgive herself for least was the conviction that Santino was a liar and a cheat when he had never been anything but honest and straight with her.

How much could she still blame Santino for effectively getting her the sack? She understood all too well his angry impatience and his need to take control when she herself seemed to have made such a hash of things. He had made it clear that if she conceived his child, he would stand by her. What good had it been for her to talk about a letter that he had never received? Had he got the chance, he would have been a part of Florenza's life from the start. And that was why he was asking her to marry

him. Her wretched pride had made her too quick to refuse that
option. After all, she loved Santino, could not imagine *ever* loving anyone else…

Fifty feet away, Santino came to a halt to study Poppy on her
log and Florenza snuggled up in her buggy. Poppy did not look
happy. The marriage proposal had not been a winner. But then
he had not promoted his own cause by depriving her of her
employment, had he? However, an ever-recurring image of
Poppy sailing away in a Brewett limo the following day never
to return had driven him to a desperate act. He had known exactly what he'd been doing, he acknowledged grimly. He had
cut the ground from beneath her feet in a manoeuvre calculated
to make her more vulnerable to his arguments.

Glancing up and seeing him, Poppy froze. Dressed in tan
chinos and a beige padded jacket that accentuated his black hair
and olive skin, Santino looked stunning. Her mouth ran dry.
Should she admit that she'd been a bit too hasty in turning him
down?

'Won't your guests miss you?' she asked as he dropped down
into an athletic crouch to look at Florenza.

'Country house guests entertain themselves and most of them
are still in bed. As long as I show up for dinner, nobody's of-
fended,' Santino told her, resting appreciative eyes on his baby
daughter. 'She's something special, isn't she?'

In a sudden decision, Poppy reached into the buggy and lifted
Florenza free of the covers. Santino vaulted upright, looking ever
so slightly unnerved. 'I've never held a baby before. It might
upset her.'

'She's a very easy-going baby. Just support her head so that
she feels secure.'

Santino cradled Florenza in careful arms. He looked down
into his daughter's big, trusting blue eyes and then he smiled, a
proud, tender, almost shy smile that made Poppy's eyes glisten.
'She's not crying. Do you think she sort of knows who I am?'

'Maybe…' Her throat was thick.

'And maybe not, but she can learn.' Santino studied Poppy
with sudden, unexpected seriousness. 'Let's hope that Florenza
never does to me what I did to my own mother. I'm in your

debt for what you said the night of the party about me having taken my father's side when my parents divorced.'

Poppy blinked. 'How in my debt?'

'I went over to Italy to see Mama and found out what a pious little jerk I'd been,' Santino admitted with a rueful grimace. 'I blamed her for the divorce and she didn't want to ruin my relationship with my father by telling me that throughout their marriage he'd had a whole string of casual affairs. I just wish he'd been man enough to admit that to me, instead of going for the sympathy vote to ensure that I chose to live with him when they broke up.'

Knowing how close he had been to his father, Maximo, Poppy muttered, 'I'm sorry…'

'No. Don't be.' Santino smiled. 'Thanks to what you said, my mother and I are getting to know each other again.'

Poppy was delighted at that news. 'That's brilliant!'

'I would never be unfaithful to you,' Santino informed her in steady continuation, and then his wide sensual mouth curved in self-mocking acknowledgement. 'I'm even working on my narrow-minded response to pink graphs…'

Poppy froze at that teasing conclusion. 'That was *you*…that emailed me the day of the party?'

'Who did you think it was?' Santino glanced at her in surprise before hunkering down to settle their sleeping daughter back into her buggy with gentle hands.

It meant so much to Poppy to know that that teasing exchange had been with him. Her heart just overflowed, and when Santino sprang back up again he was a little taken aback but in no mood to complain when Poppy flung her arms round him and hugged him. 'I think I might just want to marry you, after all,' she confided. 'Is the offer still open?'

'Very much,' Santino breathed not quite levelly, unable to drag his gaze from her happy, smiling face and absolutely terrified that she might change her mind. 'How do you feel about getting married next week in Italy?'

Her lashes fluttered up on shaken blue eyes. '*That*…soon?'

'I'm really not a fan of long engagements,' Santino swore with honest fervour.

'Neither am I,' Poppy agreed with equal conviction, her heart singing, for there was something very reassuring about a guy who just couldn't wait to get her to the altar.

CHAPTER NINE

WALKING back towards the priory, Santino said with smooth satisfaction, 'I'll feel a lot more comfortable when you sit down to dinner with my guests this evening.'

At that prospect, Poppy's eyes widened in dismay. 'But I can't do that. I came here as the Brewetts' nanny and what are people going to *think* if I suddenly—?'

'That you're my future wife with more right than most to grace the dining table.' Impervious, it seemed, to the finer points of the situation, Santino exuded galling masculine amusement.

'Well, it can't be done. I didn't bring any dressy clothes. I've got nothing but jeans!' Poppy exclaimed.

'If that's the only problem…we'll go out and get you something to wear right now, *cara mia.*'

Nothing pleased Santino so much as solving problems with decisive activity. The village a few miles away rejoiced in a very up-market boutique. It took him only twenty minutes to run Poppy there, stride in, select a short, strappy, soft blue dress off the rail, which struck him as absolutely Poppy, and herd her into the changing room, paying not the slightest attention to her breathless and shaken protests.

Inside the cubicle, Poppy stared at her reflection dreamily in the mirror and wondered how Santino had managed to pick the right size and a shade of blue that looked marvellous with her hair. Then she looked at the price tag and almost had a heart attack.

'Poppy…?' Santino prompted from the shop floor.

Poppy emerged. Santino had Florenza draped over one shoulder and looked for all the world like a male who had been dandling babies from childhood. Impervious to the sales woman oozing appreciation over him, he studied Poppy with shimmering dark golden eyes that made her cheeks fire with colour and her heart pound like a manic road drill.

'We'll take the dress,' Santino pronounced without hesitation. 'What about shoes?'

Before Poppy could part her lips Santino was requesting her opinion on the display, and within minutes she was trying a pair on. When she reappeared in her jeans, two women were clustered round Santino admiring Florenza and his deft touch with her. By the sound of the dialogue she could hear, he was showing off like mad. Both shoes and dress were removed from her grasp and paid for with Santino's credit card without her having any opportunity to speak to him in private.

'Do you have any idea how much that little lot cost?' Poppy whispered in total shock as they settled back into the limo.

Santino gave her an enquiring glance. 'No.'

Poppy told him.

Santino looked surprised. 'A real steal...'

'It's a fortune!' Poppy gasped.

'Allow me to let you into a secret,' Santino teased in the best of good humour. 'I'm not a poor man.'

Back at the priory, it was a further shock to discover that her possessions and Florenza's had been moved from the nursery wing to a magnificent guest suite on the first floor. 'Are you sure I'm supposed to be here?' she asked the butler, Jenkins.

'Of course,' he wheezed.

Poppy urged him to sit down. He looked shifty and muttered, 'You won't mention this to Mr Santino, will you?'

'Well, I...' Poppy felt the old man really ought not to be working in such a condition.

And then Jenkins explained. He lived alone and he had been in retirement for five years, but he'd missed the priory and his old profession terribly. At his own request, Santino had allowed the old man to come back to the priory and relive what he termed the good old days on occasional weekends and he very much enjoyed that break. Touched by that explanation and by Santino's understanding, Poppy said no more.

Dinner was not at all the ordeal she had imagined it might be. But then she had always enjoyed meeting new people, and from the instant she entered the drawing room and Santino's dark and appreciative gaze fell on her she also felt confident that she looked her best. Late evening, Santino came upstairs with her and went into the dressing room off her bedroom to look in on his sleeping baby daughter. His lean, dark face softened, his sensual mouth curving. 'It's extraordinary how much I feel for her already,' he confided.

A discomfiting little pang assailed Poppy and she rammed it down fast. How could she possibly be envious of the hold Florenza already had on her father's heart? After all, he was marrying her for their daughter's sake. Keen not to dwell on that painful truth, she said awkwardly, 'You know, I really can't see how we can possibly get married this coming week. It takes ages to organise even the smallest wedding.'

'The arrangements are already well in hand, *cara*,' Santino delivered with a slashing grin that made her mouth run dry. 'Early Monday morning we fly over to Venice where a selection of wedding dresses will await your choice. There is nothing that you need do or worry about. I just want you to relax and enjoy yourself.'

'It sounds like total bliss,' Poppy admitted, thinking of the weighty responsibilities and decisions that had burdened her throughout the previous year when she had had nobody to rely on but herself.

'I have a question I meant to ask you earlier,' Santino declared then. 'Exactly when last year did you write to me to tell me that you had conceived our child?'

Her brow furrowing in puzzlement, Poppy told him. His eyes flared gold and then veiled.

'What?' she prodded, unable to see the relevance of that information so long after the event.

Santino shrugged, lean, strong face uninformative. 'It's not important.'

Ultra-sensitive on that issue, Poppy was taut, and in receipt of that casual dismissal she flushed. She was convinced that he had to believe that there had never been a letter in the first place and that she was merely trying to ease her conscience and fend off his annoyance by lying and pretending that there had been. And how could she prove otherwise?

'I'm tired,' she muttered, turning away.

Lost in his own suspicions of what might have happened to that letter and determined to check out that angle as soon as he could, Santino frowned. He could not imagine what he had said to provoke the distinct chill in the air, but caution prevented him probing deeper. Once they were married, caution could take a hike, but he was determined not to risk a misstep in advance of the wedding. Saying goodnight, much as if he had only been seeing an elderly grandparent up to bed, he departed.

Disconcerted, Poppy surveyed the space where he had been and her dismayed and hurt eyes stung with hot tears. The very passionate male, who had sworn she was an irresistible temptation earlier in the day, had not even kissed her. Had that plea just been a judicious piece of flattery aimed at persuading her to marry him so that he could gain total access to Florenza? Or was he just annoyed at the idea that she might be fibbing about that wretched letter? And if that was the problem, how was she ever to convince him that she *had* written to him?

Made restive by her anxious thoughts, Poppy got little sleep and, after feeding Florenza first thing the following morning, fell back into bed and slept late. Finally awakening again, she went downstairs to find Santino surrounded by his guests. A convivial lunch followed and then the visitors began to make their departures. Only then appreciating that she still had to pack up her possessions at the Brewetts' home, Poppy slipped away to speak to her former employer and decided that it would be simplest for her to return home with them and see to the matter for herself.

'I'm catching a lift with the Brewetts to go and collect my stuff,' Poppy informed Santino at the last minute.

'I can drive you over there,' Santino offered in surprise.

'No, I thought it would be easier if I left Florenza here with you,' Poppy confided with a challenging sparkle in her gaze, although she rather suspected the female domestic staff would soon help him out with the task.

Santino was merely delighted that he would retain a hostage as it were to Poppy returning again and proud that she felt that he could be trusted. In fact, his keen mind returning to a concern that had been nagging at him all morning since he had called his secretary at her home and spoken to her, he knew exactly what he intended to do during Poppy's absence.

Three hours later, in a triumphal mode, Santino hauled his office drinks cabinet out from the wall and swept up the still-sealed and dusty envelope that lay on the carpet. He resisted the temptation to tear Poppy's lost letter open then and there. He would surprise her with it. They would open it together. Maybe that way, he would feel less bitter at the high cost of Craig Belston's mean and petty act of malice.

'If it hadn't been for you being there, I'd have hammered that little jerk,' Santino informed Florenza, where she sat strapped in her baby carrier watching him with bright, uncritical eyes. 'Then maybe not,' he acknowledged for himself in reflective continuance. 'He was so scared he *was*... I suppose I have to watch my language around you. But then you don't know any Italian curse words, do you?'

Florenza was asleep by the time he got her slotted back into the limo. Santino was really pleased with himself. He was naturally good father material, he was convinced of it. She hadn't cried once, not even when it had taken four attempts to change her and his chauffeur, a long-time parent, had mercifully intervened with a little man-to-man advice on the most effective method. They had tea at the Ritz where she was very much admired. She glugged down her bottle of milk like a trooper and concluded with a very small ladylike burp that he didn't think anyone but him heard.

'We're a real team,' Santino told Florenza on the drive home, and around then it occurred to him to wonder how Poppy planned to get herself back to the priory. With a muttered curse, he rang the Brewetts only to discover that she had already gone.

Right up until Poppy had left the Brewetts' with her cases in a taxi, she had expected Santino to call and say that he would come and pick her up. Instead she'd had to catch the train. But when she saw him waiting on the station platform to greet her at the other end of her journey, a bright, forgiving smile formed on her lips.

'I ought to grovel, *amore*,' Santino groaned in apology, looking so gorgeous that there was little that she would not have forgiven. 'It didn't even cross my mind that you don't have your own transport.'

'I expect you were too taken up with Florenza.'

'We did have quite a busy afternoon,' Santino admitted with masculine understatement. 'And when we get back to the priory, I have a surprise for you.'

The very last thing, Poppy expected was to have her own letter set before her like a prize. She was gobsmacked. 'Where on *earth* did that come from?'

'I phoned my secretary this morning. She actually remembered your letter arriving the day before she went off on holiday last year because she noticed your name on the back of the envelope. That week, *I* was in Italy mending fences with my mother.' Santino's strong jawline hardened. 'And Belston was working his last day at Aragone Systems—'

'Craig?' Poppy was still transfixed by the sight of that dusty, *unopened* letter, and her fingers were twitching to snatch it up and bury it deep somewhere Santino could never find it. At one level, she was at a total loss as to what Craig Belston could have to do with the miraculous recovery of a letter that had gone missing almost a year earlier, but on another level she was already recalling with shrinking, squeamish regret the horribly emotional outpourings of her own heart within that letter. It was wonderful how what could seem right and appropriate in the heat of the moment could then threaten utter humiliation eleven months on...

'Yes, Belston. The minute I worked out that time frame, I was suspicious. So, I called at his apartment this afternoon and was fortunate enough to find him home—'

Poppy blinked in growing disconcertion, but Santino was far too caught up in his recital to notice her taut pallor. She was cringing at that very idea of him reading that letter while she still lived and breathed. Here they were on the brink of a marriage of very practical and unemotional convenience and pride demanded that she strive to match that challenge. But he would undoubtedly die of embarrassment *for* her if he was now confronted by those impassioned pages that declared how instantly, utterly and irrevocably she had once fallen in love with him.

'I really don't know why you would've thought Craig might remember anything about one stupid letter,' Poppy muttered abstractedly, regarding the item with all the aghast intensity of a woman faced with a man-eating shark.

'He had a grudge against you and he's a coward,' Santino informed her with expressive disgust. 'I had the advantage of surprise today. He was so taken aback by the sight of Florenza and I—'

'You took Florenza with you to call on Craig?' Poppy squeaked, her expectations of Santino taking yet another beating.

'I wasn't going to leave her behind when I'd promised to take care of her,' Santino pointed out with paternal piety. 'The minute I mentioned the letter and got tough, Belston spilled the beans about what he had done with it. He threw it behind a piece of office furniture where it's been ever since. Mind you, it shows you how the cleaners cut corners.'

Poppy winced. 'What a nasty, low thing to do...oh, well, all's well that ends well and all that,' she added breathlessly, snatching up the envelope and endeavouring to scrunch its fat proportions in one hand. 'I'm glad the mystery's been solved but time has kind of made this letter redundant.'

'I still want to read it...' Questioning dark golden eyes pinned to her, Santino extended an expectant hand.

Poppy turned very pale and bit her lip and closed her other hand round the crumpled envelope as well. 'I really don't want you reading it now...'

'Why?'

As the taut silence stretched Poppy chewed at her lower lip in desperation. Santino tensed, a cool, shuttered look locking his darkly handsome features. What the hell had she written? A total character assassination directed at him? The news that she hated him for taking advantage of her naive trust and overlooking contraception and never, ever wanted to lay eyes on him again? His taut mouth set hard. Self-evidently, the letter she had penned was of the poisonous and destructive ilk.

'So I won't open it, but it's still mine,' Santino heard himself counter with harsh clarity, and no sooner had that foolish offer left his lips than he regretted it.

Intimidated by the tone of that announcement, Poppy handed over the envelope with a reluctance that he could feel. Santino smoothed it out between long, lean fingers. 'I believed that we could read this together, that you'd be pleased I had the faith to believe that you'd sent it,' he continued in angry bewilderment. 'For the first time in my life, I feel pretty damned naive!'

Most unhappy to see him in possession of what was indisputably *his* letter, Poppy lowered her head. 'It's not the sort of thing we'd want to read together,' she mumbled in considerable mortification. 'What did you say to Craig?'

'Nothing repeatable but I didn't hit him.' Santino's dark drawl was rough-edged. 'I wanted to kill him...only not in front of Florenza.'

'Oh...' Poppy was shattered by that blunt admission.

'You see, I thought he'd cost us our chance of happiness.' Santino welded his teeth back together on the rest of what he had almost said, which was that, in his volatile opinion at that instant, *she* had just done that most conclusively. There was so much he had longed to ask and learn about those months they had spent apart, and that she could not be honest about her feelings then angered him and made him feel shut out.

'We have some forms to fill out to satisfy the wedding legalities,' Santino continued grittily. 'Then I've got some calls to make.'

He didn't even laugh when she confided that her middle name was Hyacinth. Before he went off to make those phone calls, Poppy shot a glance at his grim profile and gathered all her strength to ask, 'Are you still sure about this...sure you want to go ahead and marry me?'

'Of course, I am sure.' Having fallen still at that sudden question, Santino shook her by tossing the letter back on the table in front of her. 'Keep it. As you said, the passage of time has made it redundant.'

Poppy went up to her imposing bed and cried. What had gone wrong? Where had the wonderful warmth and intimacy gone? Surely a silly, outdated letter should not create such tension between them? And she knew that she had said and done the wrong thing. Even though it would have mortified them both beyond bearing, she should have let him have that letter...

CHAPTER TEN

AT FIVE the following afternoon after an incredibly busy day, Poppy stood out on a Venetian hotel balcony entranced by the magical scenes taking place on the quays and the canal below.

A group of masked men and women in superb medieval costumes were boarding a launch outside the imposing *palazzo* opposite. A Harlequin and a Pierrot passed by in a gliding gondola, their outfits blessing them with total anonymity. On the quay, a trio of children, dressed up as a clown, a milkmaid and a comic spotty dog were whooping with delight over the firework display streaking through the heavens above the rooftops. Venice at carnival time: noisy, colourful and so full of bustling, vivid life that the very air seemed to pulse with mystery and the promise of excitement.

'You are pleased to be here with us?' A designer-clad little dynamo of a lady of around sixty, Santino's mother, Dulcetta Caramanico, emanated vivacity and natural warmth.

'I have had the most wonderful day…' Poppy admitted with sincerity. 'And I can't thank you enough for the fantastic welcome you have given us.'

Poppy had not expected to meet her future in-laws alone, but urgent business had forced Santino at the eleventh hour to accept the necessity of his coming out on a later flight. Greeted at the airport by Santino's mother and Arminio, his charming stepfather, Poppy and Florenza had been wafted on to their motor launch and across the lagoon into the city of Venice. They had brought her to their hotel but it had taken her most of the day to work out that the older couple indeed owned an entire chain of international hotels, famed for their opulence, legendary customer service and exclusivity.

From the instant Dulcetta and Arminio had laid eyes on them, Poppy and Florenza had been treated as though they were already a much-loved part of the family circle. Florenza had been the star of the party. The luxurious suite of rooms allotted to them would have been at home in a palace. That morning, the Caramanicos had taken them to St Mark's Square to see the Flight of the Little Doves that officially opened the carnival, and after lunch Dulcetta had escorted Poppy to a fantastic bridal salon where a huge array of glorious gowns and accessories had awaited her inspection.

Dulcetta was delighted by Poppy's freely expressed gratitude, and her fine dark eyes shone with happy tears. 'It is a joy to please you, Poppy. You brought my son home to me and now you are even making him smile again. When Santino first visited me last year, he didn't confide in me but I sensed how very unhappy he was at heart.'

Poppy hung her bright head, wondering how low she would sink in the popularity stakes when Santino arrived in Venice looking as grim and detached as he had the night before at the priory.

'Santino may have inherited Maximo's looks and business acumen,' his loving mother continued. 'But inside, Santino is much more emotional and caring than ever his father was. So will you wear the dress for me this evening and surprise my son?'

Poppy focused on the utterly over-the-top eighteenth-century-style silk, brocade and lace gown on the dress form that awaited her and a rueful grin tilted her generous mouth. 'Just you try and stop me getting into the carnival spirit!' She laughed in spite of her aching heart. 'It's such a fantastic outfit...'

Maybe, even if Santino believed that she looked ridiculous, he would at least smile at the effort she was making, Poppy thought when Dulcetta had left her. Tears prickled her eyes as she removed her make-up and freshened up with a bath. Only a few days before her wedding, she ought to be the happiest woman alive. After all, she was about to marry the man she loved...but a man who would not be marrying her had it not been for their daughter's birth. Santino adored Florenza though, and he would make a wonderful father. It was just selfish of her to want the moon into the bargain.

Santino had already been alienated by her foolishness over

the letter and it had finally occurred to her that he might even have got the impression that what she had written was unpleasant in some way. His unashamed anger with Craig, his belief that the other man had cost them the chance of happiness the previous year, had shaken Poppy when he'd voiced it, but at the time she had been too enervated to appreciate what Santino had *really* been telling her. Too busy conserving her pride and protecting herself from embarrassment, she had neglected to note that Santino had been making no such pretences. It shamed her that he should be so much more open and unafraid than she was. He had told her how attracted he was to her, shown her in his anger what he believed Craig Belston had stolen from them, for without his spiteful interference they might have been together much sooner...

And what had she done? Let Santino continue thinking that the valentine card had been a joke. She had saved face at every turn and given not an inch because the memory of her own adoring generosity the night of the party still mortified her. Yet it had been a wonderful night of love and sharing and wasn't it time that she acknowledged that? It didn't matter that he didn't love her. He cared, he certainly *cared*. From now on, she swore that would be enough for her.

While Poppy was anxiously owning up to her sins of omission, Santino, who had just arrived in his own suite next door, was confronting *his* as well. He needed to squash the conviction that he deserved a woman who saw him in terms of being the sun around which her world resolved. Poppy was not in love with him but that was only the beginning of the story, *not* the end. Ego might urge him to play it cool, but playing it cool was not advancing his own cause in any way, was it? For a start, he had been downright childish about that letter, he conceded with gritted teeth. Her determination to prevent him from accessing material that would damage their present relationship had been sensible. Just as Santino *still* recalled every word Poppy had affixed to that valentine card almost twelve months earlier, so he knew that he would have been haunted for ever more by the accusations he imagined had to be contained in that letter.

Anchoring the glorious feathered head-dress to her upswept

Titian hair took Poppy some time. Dulcetta and Arminio had invited her to dine with them and a maid was to come upstairs to sit with Florenza. Poppy attached the glittering diamanté-studded mask to her eyes and surveyed herself. The emerald-green gown had theatrical splendour and the neat low-cut bodice flattered her lush curves in a way that made her blush. Yet she felt her own mother would not have recognised her, a stray thought that hurt just a little for she had decided not to tell her family about her wedding until after the event. At such short notice and with flights from Australia and accommodation in Venice during the carnival being so expensive, it would have been impossible for her parents to attend their daughter's special day. But in her heart of hearts, Poppy had also feared to put what she deemed to be already strained affections to the test.

When the knock on the door sounded, Poppy hurried to answer it before Florenza, who had just gone to sleep, could awaken again.

Disconcerted that it was Santino, whom she had believed might not arrive much before midnight, she fell back an uncertain step. Intent golden eyes pinning to her, he murmured something in husky Italian and his heartbreaking smile slowly curved his handsome mouth. As ever, he looked devastatingly dark, vibrant and attractive.

Her breath caught in her throat, for she had truly wondered if Santino would ever smile at her again. Her heartbeat picked up tempo and a flock of butterflies flew free in her tummy, but she held her head high, firmly convinced he would not recognise her at first glance.

'Poppy…' Santino said without a second of hesitation.

'I thought you wouldn't know it was me!' Poppy wailed in helpless disappointment.

As he closed the door his wonderful smile deepened. 'I would know you anywhere. In any light and any disguise.'

'You'll be able to dine with your mother and stepfather, after all.' Feeling foolish, Poppy reached up and unfastened the diamanté mask to set it aside.

'No. I called them from the airport and expressed our mutual regrets.' Santino's expression was now very serious. 'We need to be alone so that we can talk.'

Poppy tensed in sudden apprehension. It was as if he had pushed a panic button. Suddenly she feared he was as keen to cancel the wedding as he had been to cancel the family dinner. 'Santino…'

'No, let me have the floor first…' Santino dealt her a taut look from his beautiful eyes, his raw tension palpable. 'I haven't been straight with you. I haven't been fair either—'

'You're stealing my lines…' Poppy sped past him to snatch up her handbag and withdraw the much-abused letter, which she thrust at him in near desperation. 'I didn't think how it must've looked when I wouldn't let you read it, but it is *your* letter—'

'Stuff the letter,' Santino groaned, not best pleased to have been interrupted just when he had got into his verbal stride and setting it straight back into her unwilling hand. 'It's unimportant. What matters is that I tell you how I feel…but you're not likely to be impressed by the news that you had blown me away in Wales before it dawned on me that I was in love with you.'

In the act of ripping in frustration into the envelope for herself to produce a thick wad of notepaper, Poppy stopped dead and viewed Santino with huge, incredulous blue eyes. She couldn't possibly have heard *that*, she told herself. In fact she must have been dreaming…

'*Porca miseria*…in advance of that day, strange as it may seem,' Santino disclaimed with touching discomfiture and a look that was a positive plea for understanding in his strained dark eyes. 'I just had no idea why I was always coming down personally to the marketing department, why the day seemed a little brighter when I saw you, why I just *liked* you, why I started finding fault with every other woman I met…have you anything to say?'

In shock, Poppy shook her head.

'Your very first day when I took you to hospital after you hurt your finger,' Santino reminded her doggedly, lean, strong features taut, 'I demonstrated how macho I was by passing out at the sight of the needle coming your way. Yet even though you were a real chatterbox and all my staff would have fallen about in stitches had you told them about that episode, you kept quiet. That was remarkably restrained of you…'

'I wouldn't have d-dreamt of embarrassing you at work.' A great rush of answering love was surging up inside Poppy and playing havoc with her speech.

'I know, *amore*…' But his shapely mouth only semi-curved. 'I was furious when my marketing head overreacted to that stupid cup of coffee. I was so protective of you, and then at the party, when Belston was scoring points off you, I could've ripped him apart! And when we were together in my office and I finally had you all to myself, it was more temptation than I was capable of withstanding—'

'I felt like I'd thrown myself at you…' Poppy shared painfully.

'Who stopped you from leaving? Who kissed you? Who made all the *real* moves?'

Only then did Poppy appreciate that the prime mover had been him. 'But you had been drinking—'

Santino groaned out loud. 'I was just making excuses for myself. That night nothing had ever felt so right to me and I knew exactly what I was doing, but the next day I felt appallingly guilty for seducing you—'

'I sneaked off because I thought it was all my fault—'

'And I was furious about that. I called round at your bedsit that afternoon—'

Poppy winced. 'Oh, no…you just missed me…'

'I suspected you were home and just not answering the door because you didn't want to see me—'

'I wouldn't have done that.'

'Then I had to phone round half of Australia to track down your sister-in-law, Karrie, to find out where you were. Didn't she tell you about my call?'

Even though her heart was singing, Poppy had paled. 'Yes, but I just assumed it was because you were really worried I might be pregnant 'cos at that stage I still believed you were engaged to Jenna. Santino…I think you ought to take a look at this letter of mine before I get so mad with myself that I scream!'

But Santino had other ideas. She was still listening and her lovely eyes were soft and warm and it had been a day and a half since he had last touched her. Tugging her into connection with his lean, powerful length, he brought his mouth swooping down with unashamed hunger and urgency on hers, and for timeless minutes she clung, every fibre of her being alive with joyful excitement and the wondrous relief of knowing herself loved.

Pausing to snatch in a ragged breath, gazing down into her shining eyes, Santino muttered, 'Sooner or later, I'll find the magic combination of making you love me back...if only you hadn't hated me when you were in Wales—'

'I didn't—'

'I was devastated for weeks after that. I tore up the belated valentine card I had searched high and low for—'

'You bought me a card?' Poppy was touched to the brink of tears.

'Signed it with an unadventurous question mark...the guy with few words. All I could think about was getting you back to London. I didn't understand I loved you until that day...'

Her throat thickened. Stepping back, she handed him the letter. 'Well, I always knew how I felt about you, but I'll forgive you for that.'

With perceptible reluctance he accepted the letter, and then as he scanned the first few lines with a frown such a stunned look began to form on his lean, strong face that she had to suppress a giggle. Suddenly he was glued to every page with total, focused concentration.

'It's a...it's a love letter...a wonderful, fantastic love letter,' Santino finally vocalised with a roughened edge to his deep voice.

'It wasn't meant to be, but when I learned I was expecting your child I wanted you to know that my card hadn't been a cheap joke—'

'I should skin you alive for having lied to me, *amore*.' But as at that point Santino was looking at her with wondering, loving intensity, she was in no danger of taking offence. 'I *still* have that card you sent me locked in my office safe. I pretended it wasn't there so that I didn't have to dump it!'

He followed that confession up with a beautiful sapphire engagement ring that took her breath away. Then he looked in on their infant daughter and smiled at her peaceful little face before he strode into his own suite next door to don the very rakish matching eighteenth-century outfit his romantic mother had laid on for his use that evening. The burgundy velvet surcoat, lace cravat and tight-fitting breeches and boots gave him an exotic and dangerous appeal that thrilled Poppy no end. For a while, all he wanted to talk about was what it had been like for her to carry their daughter during those months apart from him. Then they ended up in each other's arms again and Santino pulled back and announced that they were dining out.

'Oh…' Poppy mumbled in surprise.

'We're not going to share a bedroom until we're married, *amore mio*,' Santino swore. 'It's the only way I can *ever* hope to live down that sofa.'

So he took her out into the city where he had been born and they dined in an intimate restaurant by candlelight, both of them so busy talking, both of them so incredibly happy that they had a glow about them that drew understanding and envious eyes.

On Poppy's wedding day, the early morning mist was lifted by sunlight.

She had actually forgotten that it was Valentine's Day, but then a giant basket of beautiful flowers and a glorious card covered with roses and containing a tender verse arrived. Inside, Santino had written those three little words that meant so much to her, 'I love you', and even *signed* it. So, it started out a fantastic day that just went on getting better and better.

She had only just finished her breakfast and was feeding Florenza when someone knocked on the door and her whole family—her mother and father and Peter and Karrie and her little nephew, Sam—trooped in. She couldn't believe her eyes. Santino had flown them out at his expense and they were staying in the same hotel. He had arranged that in secrecy for her benefit and she loved him even more for that sensitivity. All the awkwardness she might have felt in other circumstances with her family evaporated straight away and, watching her mother's eyes glisten over Florenza and enveloped in a hug by her father and her brother, Poppy was content.

Her mother and her sister-in-law helped her dress, enthusing over her exquisite ivory gown with its hand-painted hem of delicate pastel roses. A magnificent tiara and drop earrings arrived with a card signed by Santino. Tucked into a velvet-lined gondola for her passage to her wedding, Poppy felt like a princess. But when she saw Santino turn from the altar in the wonderful old church, that was when her heart truly overflowed with happiness.

The reception was staged in a superb ballroom and there were masses of guests. The bridegroom and the bride were so absorbed in each other that their guests smiled and shook their heads in wonderment. They watched them dance every dance in a world of their own and then depart for their honeymoon.

Late that night in Santino's hideaway home in the wooded hills of Tuscany, Poppy lay in their incredible medieval bed draped with crewelwork drapes and surveyed her new husband with an excusable degree of satisfaction.

'Just to think you were falling in love with me all those weeks I worked for you…and I hadn't the foggiest idea.' Poppy sighed blissfully and reckoned that low self-esteem was likely to be a very rare sensation in her future.

'Neither had I,' Santino quipped, dark golden eyes resting on her with adoring intensity as he gathered her close again. 'But I missed you so much when you weren't there. I love you, *amore*.'

'I love you, too. But just to think of *me* almost breaking *your* heart, it's heady stuff—'

'You are revelling in your power,' Santino groaned in teasing reproach.

Wearing an ear-to-ear grin, Poppy nodded in agreement, for finding out that he had never, ever been in love before, no, not once, made her feel that providence had kept him safe for her. They chatted about whether or not they would return to Venice for a night or two, checked on Florenza and congratulated each other on having created such a truly wonderful baby. All too soon they melted back into each other's arms and kissed and hugged, both of them feeling as though they were the very first couple ever to discover that amount of love and revelling in their happiness.

Kim Lawrence

RAFAEL'S PROPOSAL

CHAPTER ONE

THE door of the lift was just closing when Maggie Coe slipped in.

'I've been trying to catch you all day, Rafe!' she cried breathlessly. 'I want to run something by you.'

Rafael Ransome didn't consider a lift a suitable place to conduct business conversations, especially when he was on his way home after working twelve hours straight to persuade the intransigent CEO of an ailing electronics company that awarding himself and the senior management team a fifty-per-cent pay rise while simultaneously laying off production staff wasn't the best strategy to ensure the long-term future of the firm!

Ninety-nine out of a hundred people would have been able to deduce his feelings from the discouraging expression on his striking dark features, but Maggie Coe was not one of the ninety-nine.

Rafe ran a hand over the dark stubble on his normally clean-shaven jaw and grimaced. Her tunnel vision made Maggie an asset professionally, but it was a real pain in the rear when all you wanted was a hot shower and a cold drink.

'It looks like you have me for the next sixty seconds.' Co-incidentally the same time, according to his disapproving mother, of his longest *relationship* to date.

Despite the shaky start, about thirty seconds into her pitch Maggie had his full attention.

'So effectively all she'd be doing is sorting mail.' Typically Rafe cut to the chase. 'Is that right—?'

Maggie Coe nodded, too pleased with herself to note the steely tone of disapproval that had entered his deep voice. 'And licking the odd stamp,' she added with a smile of satisfaction.

She looked up with every expectation of seeing her boss looking dumbstruck with admiration that she'd come up with the perfect solution to a troublesome problem—the problem in question being Natalie Warner, a young woman who couldn't seem to get her priorities right.

They didn't need an employee who was going to turn up late if her child had a snuffle, even if she did always scrupulously make up that lost time and more. The fact that moreover she didn't complain when she was regularly allocated an unfair proportion of the tedious, boring tasks didn't cut any ice with Maggie. As far as she was concerned, if they tolerated such a *laissez-faire* attitude they were at risk of setting a dangerous precedent, and, as she had told Mr Ransome, before long everyone would be strolling in when it suited them.

In short, anarchy.

Even though she couldn't see his expression Maggie had no doubts that a man who valued efficiency as much as Rafael Ransome, and who furthermore was capable of being as ruthless as he deemed necessary to achieve it, shared her view.

The silent lift came to a halt at the required floor, but Rafe pressed a button to prevent the door opening and turned back to the woman beside him.

'Do you not feel that opening envelopes is a waste of someone with her qualifications?' he questioned his zealous subordinate mildly. Those who knew him best would not have been fooled by the casual tone, but Maggie was blissfully blind to any signs of danger in the cold eyes or in the nerve pulsating in his lean cheek.

'Well, I'm hoping she'll think so,' came the smart reply.

Rafael's eyes narrowed thoughtfully. Maggie was prone to seeing things in terms of black and white, but she was a normally fair-minded person. Her hostility for this young woman seemed almost personal, which wasn't like her.

Natalie Warner, he reflected grimly, seemed to have a knack for aggravating people. She had certainly got under his skin...not in a personal way, of course—he made it a rule never to mix business with pleasure. It was just he hated to see talent wasted and Natalie Warner had buckets of the stuff, even though she seemed determined not to use it.

'So you're hoping that she'll be humiliated and resign...?' A child could have seen exactly what Maggie's tactics were.

'That's her choice, but let's just say I wouldn't try and stop her.'

She sounded so complacent that it took Rafe several seconds to control the sharp flare of fury that washed over him. It was ironic that the person on whose behalf he felt so angry wouldn't have felt even slightly grateful if she'd known she had aroused his dormant protective instincts.

An image of a heart-shaped face floated in the air before his eyes, a rare distracted expression entered the densely blue—some said cold—eyes of the man who was famed for his single-minded focus. Natalie Warner barely reached his shoulder and looked as fragile as delicate china, but the likeness was highly deceptive. Any man whose chivalrous instincts were aroused by her appearance would be well advised to repress them unless he fancied an earful of abuse for his efforts—he'd seen her in action and had felt sympathy for the man foolish enough to imagine she needed any special favours.

Rafe admired independent, spunky females—*admired* but avoided involvement with. At this point in his life he wasn't into high-maintenance relationships. But Natalie Warner wasn't just self-reliant, she was the sort of prickly, pigheaded female who wouldn't have asked for a glass of water if she were on fire just to make a point.

'Have you considered that she could have a good case of constructive dismissal if she wanted to take it farther?'

Maggie quickly assured him she had covered this. 'Her job title will be the same, and there will be no drop in her salary. The content of her job would even be the same on paper.' The older woman shrugged. 'So she can't claim she's been demoted.'

'This is in fact a sideways move,' Rafael mused drily.

'Exactly.'

So much for the sisterhood he was always hearing about. 'It doesn't bother you that she's a single parent with a child?'

This time even Maggie couldn't miss the steel in his voice. She blanched as his long lashes lifted from the sharp angles of his razor-sharp slanting cheekbones to reveal disapproval glittering in his deep-set eyes.

'*Bother me?*' she echoed, evincing confusion while she did

some fast thinking. It was becoming clear that, far from being pleased with her ingenuity, Rafe was inexplicably furious—in that quiet but devastating way he had. 'In what way?' she questioned, desperately trying to retain her composure in the face of the displeasure of a man she deeply admired and whose approval she craved.

'Don't play the innocent with me, Maggie,' he drawled, an expression of simmering impatience stamped on his classically handsome features.

'You say yourself that there's no room for sentimentality in the workplace,' she reminded him with a hint of desperation.

'I rather think you might be taking that quote out of context,' he returned drily.

Maggie flushed. 'So you want her to stay where she is?'

Do I…?

Ironically his life would be a lot more comfortable if he let Maggie install the distracting thorn in his side in some dark cupboard. He sighed; as tempting as it was, he couldn't let her do it. God, sometimes he wished he weren't a good guy.

'You will not hide Natalie Warner away in some God-forsaken back room, Maggie.' Firmly he spelt out his instructions so there would be no convenient misunderstandings. 'Neither will you move her anywhere without my *personal* say-so.' He saw the alert expression appear on Maggie's face and wished he had omitted the *'personal'*. The last thing he wanted was that sort of rumour starting up again.

A while after Natalie had started at Ransome it had come to his attention that there had been whispers that he'd been taking a particular interest in their smart new recruit. He blamed himself for not having foreseen his actions could have been interpreted that way—he knew all too well how people's minds worked.

He could still remember the hurt look of surprise on her face when she'd come to him excited by an idea she'd had, and he had cut her dead—he had made sure there had been plenty of people to witness the snub. It had been a case of being cruel to be kind. Even if the affair had been fictitious, the rumour that she had made it, not on talent, but because she was sleeping with the boss, would haunt a woman through her career.

'You will carry on treating her exactly the same way you do all the other trainees,' he elaborated quietly. 'Do I make myself clear—?' He lifted one brow questioningly and the woman beside him gulped and nodded.

Having made his point, he allowed the door to open and stood aside to let her pass. 'Incidentally,' he called after her, 'there's a meeting scheduled next month to discuss flexible working hours.' Or at least there would be once he'd asked his PA to organise it. 'You might like to ask around to see what the level of interest would be in a crèche.'

The last of Natalie's co-workers had left an hour earlier, laughingly predicting how many valentine's cards they would receive.

'Are you doing anything special, Nat?' asked the young woman who had just boasted that her boyfriend had booked them a table at a really swish restaurant—and was pretty sure he was going to propose.

'I'm going to a wedding,' Natalie explained.

'How romantic, getting married on Valentine's Day!' someone exclaimed enviously.

Then someone else asked the question Natalie had hoped they wouldn't.

'Anyone we know, Nat?'

'Mike, my ex-husband, is getting married to his girlfriend, Gabrielle Latimer…the actress.'

'Your *ex*!'

'Oh, God, she's *gorgeous*!' someone else breathed, only to be elbowed by the guy standing beside her.

'Personally,' someone else remarked, 'I don't think she'll age well—now, if she had *your* cheekbones, Nat…' Everyone looked at Natalie and nodded. 'And I read the other day she's had a boob job.'

Natalie smiled. She appreciated the loyal attempt to make her feel better but, like the others, she knew that when it came to looks she couldn't even compete in the same league as the younger girl.

Natalie would have actually preferred to spend Valentine's Day having root-canal work than attending the wedding of the century, but her daughter, Rose, who was to be a bridesmaid, had flatly refused to attend if Mummy wasn't there, too.

At least Luke would be there for moral support.

With a sigh she set about reducing the pile of paper on the desk. When half an hour later Luke Oliver put his good-looking blond head around the partition that separated her from the rest of the large office she had made good inroads into the backlog.

'You're working late, Luke,' she observed as the rest of his body followed suit.

'I'm not the only one—after Brownie points?' he teased lightly.

'There wouldn't be any point, would there?' Natalie felt guilty when Luke looked embarrassed by her dry observation. 'I'm making up for a late start,' she admitted hurriedly. 'Rose had another asthma attack last night.' Natalie pinned an upbeat smile on her face as Luke's good-looking face creased with sympathy. 'Fortunately I managed to get her an early appointment at the doctor's this morning, but they were running late and by the time I'd finally got her settled with Ruth it was almost eleven.'

'How is she?'

'She's loads better this morning, thanks.' Even so it had torn Natalie apart to leave her fragile-looking daughter. It was a guilt thing, of course. Rose had been more than happy to stay with Ruth, who doted on her and was more than capable to cope with any crisis.

'So now you're working twice as hard as everyone else to prove you don't expect any special favours just because you're a single mum,' Luke suggested perceptively.

Natalie gave a rueful smile and rotated her head to relieve the tension in her neck and shoulders. 'You know me so well, Luke.'

Luke's glance dropped to the delicate, clear-cut features lifted to him—features made nonetheless attractive by dark smudges of fatigue under the wide-spaced, darkly lashed hazel eyes and lines of strain around the wide, softly curving lips.

'Not as well as I'd like...' he sighed huskily.

Natalie's smile morphed into a wary frown as she registered the suggestive warmth in his expression; she'd thought they'd got past all that stuff. 'You know that I'm not...' she began wearily.

Luke sighed and held up his hand. 'Sorry, I know I said I wouldn't go there, Nat, but...' his attractive smile flashed out '...you might change your mind?'

'No, I won't change my mind.' Natalie hardened her heart against Luke's hurt puppy-dog look. 'And anyway, you know as well as I do that office romances never work.' She smiled to lessen her rejection. 'Besides, there's no room in my life for a man.' Or for that matter much for anything but work and sleep, and not too much of the latter when Rose wasn't well!

'Have you told little Rose yet about Mike moving to the States?'

Natalie rubbed the faint worried indentation between her feathery eyebrows and shook her head. 'Nope. I suppose I should before the wedding?' What am I doing asking a childless bachelor advice on child-rearing when I already know the answer? she thought begrudgingly. 'But I just don't know how she's going to react.' *Liar!* She knew Rose would react like any other five-year-old when she learnt the dad who spoilt her rotten every other weekend—when he turned up—was moving halfway around the world—*badly*!

Luke shifted uncomfortably. 'Actually it's about the wedding I wanted to have a word, Nat.'

His next words confirmed that the shiver of apprehension snaking down her spine was justified.

'I hate to do this to you, but Rafe has put me on the Ellis account; he's sending me to New York for a couple of weeks.' He tried to sound casual about this amazing opportunity and failed miserably.

'Congratulations.'

'Thanks, Nat. It should be you that's going, though.'

Natalie shook her head and pinned on a smile. Only a real cow would begrudge someone as nice and genuinely talented as Luke a break like this. 'You deserve it, Luke,' she assured him warmly.

'I'm afraid it means...'

'You won't be able to come to the wedding with me,' she

completed, unable to totally disguise her dismay behind a sunny smile. 'That's fine, don't worry,' she added stoically.

She wasn't surprised that Luke had said yes; when Rafe *asked* hungry young executives like Luke they never said no. In fact, she brooded, people in general don't say no to him...*except me*.

These days she didn't rate cosy chats with His Lordship, as the blue-blooded heir to a baronetcy was called—sometimes affectionately, sometimes not!—behind his back. Which just proves, she told herself wryly, that there is a bright side to having a career that's going nowhere.

On paper she and Luke had the same qualifications, they had even begun working at the top-notch management consulting firm within weeks of one another, but ten months on Luke had his own office and she was still sitting at the same desk doing routine stuff that she could have done asleep.

Things weren't likely to get better either. You didn't get offered a chance at Ransome twice and Natalie had, after much soul-searching, refused hers. Luke, who hadn't had to weigh his desire for promotion against the problems of child care, had not said no to his.

The rest, as they said, was history. She'd made her choice; she didn't consider herself a victim—lots of women managed to have high-flying careers and babies. Clearly she didn't have what it took.

'God, Nat, I'm really sorry.'

'It's not your fault,' Natalie soothed a guilty-looking Luke. 'It's *that* man,' she breathed, venom hardening her soft voice as she contemplated the grim prospect of attending the marriage of her ex to the glamorous Gabby without the support of a passable male to give the ego-bolstering illusion she had a well-rounded life. 'I don't suppose it even occurs to Rafael Ransome that some people actually have a life outside this place!'

'*Nat*, he's not that bad.'

'*Bad!* The man's a cold-blooded tyrant! I'm surprised he doesn't make us sign our contracts in blood,' she retorted with a resolute lack of objectivity. 'Forget all that stuff you read about him in the glossy supplements,' she advised Luke, imaginatively expanding her theme. 'He might have turned this place into one of the top management consulting firms in Europe virtually overnight—the success of the nineties…'

To Luke's amusement she proceeded to dismiss one of the most spectacular financial successes of the decade with a disdainful sniff.

'And have every top company beating a path to his door, but I've always reckoned he was born in the wrong century.'

Luke looked amused. 'Sounds like you've given the subject some thought?'

'Not especially,' Natalie responded hurriedly. 'It's just obvious that underneath the designer suits—'

'You've not given that much thought either, I suppose.'

'Most certainly not!' Natalie denied, insulted by the suggestion she was in the habit of mentally undressing her boss.

'*Sure* you haven't. So what *do* you think goes on under his designer suits, Nat?'

'I think there lurks the soul of a feudal, your-fate-is-in-his-hands type of despot. I can just see him now grinding the odd handful of peasants into the ground.'

Her voice lost some of its crisp edge as an intrusive mental image to match her words flashed into her head. In her defence, Rafe Ransome, his well-developed muscular thighs covered by a pair of tight and most likely historically inaccurate breeches, was enough to put the odd weak quiver into the most objective of females' voices.

Unlike Natalie, most women were not normally objective about her employer's looks; his mingled genes—Italian on his mother's side and Scottish on his aristocratic father's side—had given the man an entirely unfair advantage in the looks stakes.

'*Nat!*'

Natalie was too caught up in her historical re-enactment to hear the note of warning. 'On his way to burn down his neighbours' castle and ravish the local maidens…'

Like the modern-day equivalent, his victims probably wouldn't have put up much of a fight, she thought, contemplating with disapproval the inability of her own sex to see beyond a darkly perfect face of fallen angel and an in-your-face sensuality.

It struck her as ironic, when you considered he was set to inherit a centuries-old title and the castle that went with it from his Scottish father, that Rafael Ransome, all six feet three of him—and most of it solid muscle—looked Latin from the top of his perfectly groomed glossy head to the tips of his expressive tapering fingers.

Even she, who wasn't into dark, dynamic, brooding types, had to admit that if you discounted his disconcertingly bright electric-blue eyes Rafael looked like most women's idealised image of a classic Mediterranean male. Dark luxuriant hair that gleamed blue-black in some lights, golden skin stretched tautly over high chiselled cheekbones, and a wide, sensually moulded mobile mouth...just thinking about the cruel contours caused a shudder to ripple through her body and she hadn't even got to his lean, athletic body!

'Natalie!'

It was Luke's strangled whisper that finally made her lift her unfocused angry eyes from the computer screen, filled by now with row after row of angry exclamation marks.

Oh, God!

Even before Natalie heard the inimical deep mocking drawl the back of her neck started to prickle and her stomach gave a sickly lurch. Why, she wondered despairingly, hadn't her selective internal radar, selective as in it only spookily zapped into life when His Lordship was in the vicinity, kicked in a few moments earlier?

Her wide eyes sent an agonised question to Luke, who almost imperceptibly nodded.

I must have done something really terrible in a previous life, she thought.

CHAPTER TWO

'EMPLOYMENT law being what it is these days, I generally have to satisfy myself with the odd formal written warning, Ms Warner.'

As an alternative to ravishment?

The unbidden image that accompanied her maverick and fortunately silent response made Natalie's skin prickle with heat. She shook her head slightly as if to physically dislodge the breathless, tight feeling that made her head buzz. Being ravished, even hypothetically, by the owner of the most blatantly sensual lips she was ever likely to see was somewhere Natalie was not going.

'See you, Nat! And good luck,' Luke hissed.

And I'll need it, she thought wistfully, watching Luke making one of the fastest exits she'd ever seen—discretion obviously being the better part of valour as far as he was concerned, and who could blame him?

Still, at least there would be nobody to see her grovel, she thought dully. She took a deep breath and, squaring her slender shoulders, resolutely pushed aside a tide of self-pity that threatened to engulf her—she only had herself to blame. If you were going to bad-mouth your boss a sensible person took a few basic precautions first, such as checking he wasn't within hearing distance!

I can do humble...I *can* do humble, she silently mouthed. Even, she mentally added, if it chokes me! If I feel myself getting bolshy all I have to do, she told herself, is think about that enormous electricity bill I found sitting on the doorstep yesterday.

Maybe she was worrying over nothing—for all she knew he might see the funny side to this. Did dynamic workaholics have a sense of humour?

Gripping the arm rests of her chair so hard her knuckles turned white, she slowly swivelled her chair and raised a weak smile. Underneath she felt the same prickly feeling of antagonism she always did when in his vicinity.

'Oops! You weren't meant to hear that.' She heard with dismay a high-pitched giggle emerge from her lips. You're meant to be upbeat, not manic, she berated herself silently. God, why do I always act like a total idiot when he's around? Perhaps it was a case of doing what he expected? His attitude said he expected her to do something stupid, and she generally obliged—even if it was only tripping over her own feet!

Rafe, his beautiful mouth set in a stern straight line, raised one dark, slanted brow; beneath his heavy, half-closed lids his eyes glittered like cold blue steel. He was looking down his aristocratic nose at her because, along with the fearfully smart brain and the incredible film-star looks, Rafael Ransome was also arrogant and élitist. With his pedigree, she reflected sourly, it was not to be wondered at.

The silence was shredding her nerve endings. If he didn't say something soon she might start confessing to stuff she hadn't done! Say something even if it is sneery and sarky, she quietly muttered to herself.

Her wish was almost immediately granted.

'Such flights of fantasy, Ms Warner...' he drawled in a voice that was both sneery and sarky enough to satisfy the most demanding consumer. 'Should you ever decide to commit them to paper I have a publisher friend who would be happy to cast a professional eye over them.'

Was that his way of saying she was in the wrong job? No, a brutal 'you're not up to it' was more his style.

'I really don't think they'd be that interesting,' she replied, quieting a fresh spasm of panic... *Fantasy*, he said—he couldn't possibly know about the dreams. She broke out in a cold sweat just thinking about him being privy to her nocturnal fantasies. Not that she was going to start feeling guilty—a girl couldn't be responsible for her subconscious.

'Though if I'm going to be cast in the role of villain, litigation-wise it might be a sensible precaution if you changed a few details. Change of eye colour, make me a blond...'

Giving his character a hint of human warmth would definitely work, she thought grimly—then *nobody* would recognise him! 'It was a joke,' she insisted hoarsely.

Though if anyone had been born to fulfil the role of a ruthless criminal, she decided, sneaking a covert look through her lashes at his cold, classic profile, this was the man—it didn't require much imagination to picture him in the role of the cold-eyed assassin who aimed a gun at his victim's heart without any sign of emotion. Her own heart, perhaps in sympathy for the phantom victim, began to behave in an erratic manner, which made her feel breathless and a little light-headed.

'If you find me such an oppressive monster,' he mused, ignoring her hoarse interjection, 'I'm surprised you're still with us.'

Appealing to his sense of humour had always been a long shot.

'And at such a late hour, too...' He glanced pointedly at the metal watch on his wrist. Natalie was almost as conscious of the light dusting of dark hair on his sinewed forearm as she was of the sarcasm in his voice. Her stomach did a slow backward flip. 'Such dedication...'

She felt the colour deepen in her already pink cheeks, the sarcastic implication that she did what she had to and nothing more had enough truth in it to make her angry and defensive.

'I do what you pay me for,' she returned, successfully keeping her growing antipathy from her voice. Her control didn't stretch as far as her eyes but her antagonism did—it shone brightly in the clear depths.

This fact was not lost on Rafe, who was not displeased by the results of his calculated baiting. He reasoned that she'd eventually have to defend herself and then he might finally learn the real reason that she'd knocked back his promotion offer. He hadn't swallowed the lame 'I don't feel I'm ready' for a second.

'And not a jot more,' he completed smoothly.

Natalie's bosom swelled; smug, hateful pig! It was becoming increasingly difficult to recall her resolve to take what he threw at her and smile. I'd like to see him cope with the demands of a child and work for just twenty-four hours, she challenged mentally, allowing her gaze to sweep with simmering resentment over his tall, immaculate figure.

She exhaled noisily and tried to take control of her erratic breathing.

'Have you had any complaints about my work?' she demanded, quietly confident on this point at least. Sure, she was frequently frustrated by her inability to put more hours in at the workplace, but she also knew that she actually contributed as much and more than other people doing the same job as herself—she earned her salary.

Something that looked like amusement appeared in his eyes but it was gone so quickly and it seemed so unlikely that Natalie assumed she'd been imagining it.

'On the contrary.' One corner of his mobile mouth dropped as his eyes moved over her tense figure. 'Everyone goes out of their way to cover for you.'

In reality the simple fact was that if Natalie Warner's work hadn't been adequate she wouldn't still be at Ransome. Margaret had been right about one thing: Rafe was not sentimental about such things—when such a lot had been riding on his making a success of Ransome, he couldn't afford to be.

Quite a few people had known his own father had been behind the damaging rumours that had circulated just after the launch of Ransome, but he was the only one who knew the reason behind the old man's actions.

'If you're so damned confident how about a wager?' James Ransome had suggested when his only son had remained unmoved by the direst of his threats. 'Put your money where your mouth is, boy. If you don't make a go of it within twelve months you'll quit this nonsense and come home to run the estate.'

'Twelve months!'

'Well, if you don't think you're up to it, boy?'

Failure had not been an option.

When he looked at Natalie Warner, he saw potential going to waste—actually it wasn't the only thing he saw, but it was the only thing that had any relevance in the workplace.

'I don't need anyone to cover for me,' she gritted.

'Don't get me wrong, you're to be congratulated.' Natalie's

teeth clenched at the patronising drawl, which it seemed to her he kept just for her and bad weather. 'Overplaying the single-parent card could have caused resentment amongst your childless colleagues, but you seem to have the balance just right…plucky, but fragile.'

Not so fragile that she couldn't land a pretty good punch if you stepped out of line—she sure as hell looked as if that was what she wanted to do right now. At least that would be some sort of reaction, and preferable to the meek and mild, fade-into-the-background, yes-sir-no-sir attitude she had adopted even before she'd refused the promotion offer.

The line between his dark brows deepened as he compared this Natalie with the one who had arrived bubbling with enthusiasm and raw talent, displaying a fresh and exciting approach and causing ripples with her willingness to speak out of turn.

The sheer injustice of his accusation stunned Natalie into silence. Chin up, she met his scornful scrutiny head-on and refused to respond to the provocation. To her surprise it was Rafe who dropped his gaze first.

'For God's sake, woman,' he snapped irritably. 'You look terrible. Do you even own a mirror?'

Aware that her automatic female response to his criticism had been to lift a hand to her hair, Natalie frowned and pulled it angrily back to her lap. Rafe Ransome thinks I'm a dog… This should come as no great surprise—she'd seen the type he dated. A man who could probably emerge from a hurricane without a hair out of place was never going to feel anything but disgust for someone who looked messy as soon as she walked out of the door.

The unexpected urge she felt to burst into tears just went to prove she had more vanity left than she had thought.

'Well, you've no room to talk!' Rafe looked so astounded by her sharp retort that Natalie almost laughed. It was probably the first time in his life anyone had implied there was any fault in his appearance. He might be a nicer person if they had, *and* he might be a little more tolerant of those who didn't possess his physical perfection—like her!

'When did you last shave?' she demanded with a disdainful

nod towards the dark, incriminating shadow. Actually the look of dangerous dissipation it lent him was not unattractive.

Rafe lifted a hand to his jaw and looked amused. 'I had an early start,' he admitted.

'That's fine, because *I* don't judge people on appearances,' she informed him piously. 'And, just for the record, I hardly think my looks or lack of them are relevant to my ability to do my job.' And until you drew attention to it I hadn't even thought about the way I looked, she thought, angling a look of seething dislike up at his face.

Not true, the irritating voice of honesty in her head piped up— you started thinking about the way you looked the moment you saw him. It was at times like this, she thought with a sigh, that self-deception was infinitely preferable to the truth. Not that there was any sinister significance in her bizarre reactions to his presence, neither was it unique she'd seen the way other women in the building acted when he was around—God, but it must be awful to be married to someone all other women regarded with lust.

Oh, sure, Nat, a fate worse than death!

Just because you caught yourself wondering what undies you'd put on that morning when you saw a man didn't mean you were contemplating him or anyone else seeing them. Rafe was the sort of man who would be pretty knowledgeable when it came to women's underwear, she mused…or at least removing them. He was just the sort of man that made women conscious that they were…well…women! Possibly because he was so obviously and in-your-face *male*!

'Granted, but your ability to do your job is compromised if you're too tired and run-down to work and an ill-kempt appearance is hardly professional.' Neither was it professional for him to want to unfasten the piece of velvet ribbon that held the hair she'd scraped back from her face in an unattractive ponytail.

Natalie, teeth clenched and head bent over her desk, was unaware that her boss was finding the exposed nape of her neck strangely attractive. Calling her physically repulsive was one thing, but calling her unprofessional really hurt, especially when his accusation had some foundation. Uncomfortably she glanced down at her crumpled skirt and the run in her tights; he was right, she was a complete mess!

'Linen is meant to look crumpled.'

'If crumpled was the look you were after, congratulations, you've succeeded.'

Though she looked as though she'd been dragged through a hedge backwards, her nut-brown hair looked smooth and glossy. Rafe felt confident that it would feel like silk if he let it fall through his fingers.

'Are you wearing *any* make-up…?' he rasped suddenly, exhibiting what seemed to her to be a peculiar preoccupation with her appearance.

'I'm not sure,' she responded without thinking. She found this conversation, like his critical scrutiny, was getting far too personal for her taste.

'You're not sure!' he ejaculated, looking at her with the sort of expression she suspected he reserved for females without lipstick and Martians.

'Did someone die and make you the style police? Or is it now office policy not to appear without lip gloss?' she grunted with a belligerent frown.

He shook his head. 'Don't be ridiculous!' he snapped impatiently.

She wasn't even beautiful, he thought, examining the too-sharp contours of her pale, pinched face. Actually, though her features lacked symmetry they did have a certain charm and her smooth skin, though as pale as milk, was amazingly blemishless. So she was attractive, he conceded, but beautiful—no, and either she had no fashion sense at all or for perverse reasons known to her alone she went out of her way to wear things that didn't suit her. Take today's offering, for instance…he looked and barely repressed a shudder.

Natalie hunched her shoulders and lifted her chin as she registered the pained expression on his dark, saturnine features. She could have explained that she'd had things other than colour co-ordinating her outfit on her mind that morning. Things such as hoping Rose wouldn't end up being hospitalised *again*, but that explanation would no doubt elicit another accusation of her using her daughter to get special treatment—and no way was she going to give the smug ratbag the satisfaction.

Is it against your precious principles to say something that might make him *not* want to dispense with your services? Or is an apology too much like good sense? the exasperated voice in her head pondered.

'I'm sorry you heard what I said. I was upset...'

'Sorry I heard, or sorry you said it?'

Rafe, it seemed, was not in the mood to be placated.

She eyed him with escalating irritation. 'Well, if you're going to be pedantic...' She closed her eyes as she heard the snippy words slip from her lips. God, I'm doing it again! She opened her eyes and pinned a bland smile on her face. 'I wasn't being serious, it's just Luke had just told me something a bit upsetting.'

'I'm so sorry that work interferes with your social life.' Natalie's bewildered eyes locked with his; the depth of smouldering anger in the deep, drowning blue only deepened her confusion. She couldn't imagine what had put it there. 'You weren't happy Luke was going to New York...' he reminded her in a terse, clipped voice. 'Couldn't you bear to be parted from him that long?'

'You were standing there all that time!' she gasped without thinking. 'Well, I call that plain sneaky not letting on,' she told him indignantly.

She was actually more indignant than she might have been because there was a grain of truth in what he'd said. Of course she was pleased for Luke's good fortune, but she could still guiltily recall the wave of shameful envy that she'd felt for a split second when Luke had told her his news.

For a moment he looked taken aback by her indignant cry, then she saw his electric-blue eyes fill with laughter. His mobile lips twitched, and Natalie, who normally had no problem laughing at herself, especially when she said something spectacularly stupid—and that little gem *definitely* qualified—felt more inclined to lie on the floor and scream.

'I wasn't actually trying to hide and if you hadn't been so

absorbed by pulling my character to shreds you would have seen
me...or at least seen the message Luke was desperately trying
to signal.'

The mention of Luke reminded Natalie of his original accusation. 'I was not upset because you gave Luke a great job!' At
least the notion that she had a social life at all was funny. 'And
I'm happy for him,' she insisted sturdily.

Even as she spoke she saw herself, not Luke, striding confi-
dently into the New York office. Even Rafael would have found
no fault with this glossily groomed other her, she thought, releasing the image. A realist, she was impatient with herself for
indulging in this romanticised daydream.

'If you don't mind a little bit of advice?' Rafe suggested,
watching the revealing expressions flit across her face with narrowed eyes.

'Do I have any choice?'

She instantly regretted her childish retort as his perfect profile
hardened with displeasure. Do you actually want to lose your
job, Natalie? The problem with men like Rafe, she told herself,
was they could dish it out, but, surrounded by people who con-
stantly told them how marvellous they were, they bleated foul
if anyone gave it back.

'I think that it's possible you might find that your relationship
with Luke would stand a better chance in the long term if you
actually support his efforts to promote his career rather than
trying demotivate him.' The condescension in his voice made
her teeth ache and her fingers furl into combative fists. 'Some
people are not happy to drift along without any real challenge.'

No need for him to add that he considered her one of this
breed he evidently despised when the scornful expression on his
dark features said all too clearly he thought she was.

'How dare you?' His smug, sanctimonious attitude made her
long to beat her hands against his broad chest, though he'd probably emerge from the attack without a hair out of place and
she'd have bruised fists and no job!

Quivering, she rose to her feet; even then she barely reached
Rafael's broad shoulder. As their eyes locked a wave of dizziness hit her, making the room tilt and everything but his dark,

devastating features shift out of focus... They seemed to sharpen until they filled her vision; similarly the subtle male scent of his body filled her nostrils...

'Are you ill?'

Only in the head. Natalie closed her eyes and took a deep, fortifying breath. Actually this close it wasn't possible to pretend even to herself that the damage was restricted to her mental capacity, not when her body started responding in some very embarrassing ways to the man.

She had no illusions, she could have dressed up the effect he had on her in all sorts of painless ways, but what would be the point? It wouldn't change anything. He was an outrageously attractive, sexy guy—in a dark, predatory way that wasn't to her taste, at least not on an intellectual level. Problem was it wasn't her intellect that was in action here, it was her indiscriminate hormones that were responding to his raw animal magnetism.

She could be a victim of her hormones or she could rise above them.

Her knees were trembling—in fact her entire body was quivering as she tried to shake off the last remnants of the red blur before her eyes.

'If I did have a relationship with Luke, which I don't—*I don't!*—' she enunciated grimly from between gritted teeth in response to his blatantly sceptical smile '—the last person I'd take advice from would be someone with the emotional depth of a puddle! Luke is my friend.'

'But he'd like to be more?' He scanned her face as if he suspected to find a guilty secret written there.

CHAPTER THREE

NATALIE'S jaw tightened as she glared at Rafe belligerently. 'Would that be so amazing?' She was too angry to wonder at the personal comments coming from someone who was not exactly a touchy-feely boss. You did your job and didn't bring your personal problems to work at Ransome. 'Well, maybe he doesn't have *your* high standards!' she snarled waspishly.

The faces and figures of the women in Rafe's life could have been neatly superimposed by a computer on top of one another with no overlapping edges. Long, leggy and decorative, even the ones who weren't looked like models. Thinking about them made Natalie feel unaccountably angry.

'Or maybe he doesn't know a lost cause when he sees one,' Rafael suggested provocatively.

Natalie's nostrils flared as she took a wrathful breath. 'As for me being happy with a job that I could do in my sleep...*you think I like that*?' she quavered incredulously.

His wide shoulders lifted as he leaned towards her and his compelling eyes collided with hers before dropping to her quivering lips. He swallowed, working the muscles in his brown throat. 'Tell me what you would like,' he instructed tersely.

Tell me what you would like?

In her mind Natalie heard those words spoken in a way that changed their meaning dramatically. Her soft lips parted as a sigh snagged in her dry throat. Mike had never asked her what she'd wanted, and even if he had—an unimaginable scenario!—she doubted she could have told him. There had always been a restricting self-consciousness in the physical side of their relationship.

Natalie had sometimes wondered a little wistfully if the mind-blowing sex of legend, the sort where you forgot where you ended and your lover began, actually existed. She had come to the conclusion that if it did she was not likely to experience it.

Self-awareness was a good thing, but it was still dreadfully depressing to acknowledge that you were just too inhibited to ever experience the pleasures of head-banging, no-holds-barred sex.

Though he hadn't come right out and said so, Mike had managed to reinforce this belief with the few things he'd casually let slip about his vastly improved love life with the sexually insatiable Gabby. It was impossible to avoid coming to the inevitable conclusion that the fault must lie with her.

I'm just not a sexy, throw-caution-to-the-wind woman, which is probably why I married the first man I slept with who was my childhood sweetheart to boot!

She sighed, a dreamy expression drifting into her eyes as they dwelt speculatively on the strong features of the man who had spoken...the sensual curve of his mouth did not suggest he was overly encumbered with inhibitions. Looking at it made her breathing quicken and her tummy muscles quiver in a painfully pleasurable way.

Would Rafael be the sort of lover who would...?

With a horrified gasp Natalie pulled a veil across that dangerous line of speculation. Her neatly trimmed nails pressed half-moons into the soft flesh of her palms when, despite her best efforts, tantalising little glimpses of what lay behind that veil kept intruding in a deeply distracting manner.

In an angry gesture she flicked her head, sending her pony-tail whooshing silkily backwards. 'So that's what *this* is about!' she cried contemptuously.

Rafe watched, his blue eyes unwillingly held captive as her explosive action dislodged several more silky strands of hair from her pony-tail. If he had his way she'd never tie her hair back but wear it loose. In his mind he saw it lying straight and fine down her narrow, naked back almost reaching a waist he could span with his hands—though to know this for sure he'd have to put the theory to the test...

He cleared his throat and reached up to loosen the tie at his throat. 'Define "this".'

As if he didn't know! Maybe it was time they got this out in the open even if it did mean she lost her job.

'I turned down that stupid offer of fast-track promotion...'

she continued carelessly, brushing a stray section of hair off her face with the back of her hand. She could see a vee of brown skin where he'd undone the top button of his shirt. She ran her tongue over the dry outline of her lips as she watched his long brown fingers release the second button.

She released her baited breath in a gusty sigh as the fabric parted.

And I'm the one who always wondered what women get from watching men strip…hell, I'm getting hot and bothered over an innocent extra square centimetre of bare flesh! I've clearly lost it.

'Stupid…?' Rafael shrugged. 'I suppose,' he conceded wryly, 'in retrospect it was stupid, but at the time I actually thought I was giving you an opportunity most people in your situation dream about.'

His scornful tone made her flush angrily. 'Out of the goodness of your heart, no doubt,' she sneered irrationally—since when had business been about kindness? 'What was I meant to do with a young child when I got the word to hotfoot it to New York like Luke…shove her in my hand luggage?'

Rafe looked taken aback by her aggressive question. The line between his dark brows deepened as he shook his head. 'If *that* was the only problem why didn't you say so at the time?'

Only problem? That he could imply she was making a fuss about nothing added insult to injury.

'Why? So you could tell me you're not a social worker.' That had been Maggie's response when she had attempted to explain her dilemma to the other woman. She had gone on to warn Natalie that Mr Ransome would not be interested in her lame excuses either.

You girls these days expect it all ways. Natalie had been deeply humiliated by the contemptuous criticism; she had vowed never to give anyone the opportunity to level that accusation at her again.

His dark brows knitted. 'Social worker?' he repeated, looking genuinely perplexed. 'Being a single parent is hardly so unusual these days, is it? In fact,' he added drily, 'it's almost the norm. Half the people I know are on their second or third marriage.'

But not him. Rafe seemed one of those men who were allergic to marriage. 'More fool them.'

'You sound bitter,' he observed.

'I'm not bitter, just cautious,' she countered.

'Cautious about what?' he persisted. 'Men or marriage?'

'One is a nice idea, the other…well, just look at yourself.' The righteously indignant expression faded from her face as she followed her own advice. She stifled an appreciative sigh; he really was the *most* stunningly perfect male imaginable.

'Me…?'

'Well everyone knows you have the staying power of a two-year-old when it comes to women. Yet I suppose one day you'll meet the *right* woman and get married,' she predicted sourly. 'It's just not logical to suppose that your personality will change overnight…' Her voice faded as she encountered the blankly astonished expression on his face. It occurred to her that her evangelical enthusiasm for the subject had made her go too far. 'Well, it seems that way to me anyhow…' she added with a touch of husky defiance.

Rafe inhaled deeply and rocked back on his heels. 'So it *seems* to you I am a shallow womaniser, who will sleep with the maid of honour at my own wedding.' Cold ice scanned her dismayed face. 'Have I got that right…?' he enquired in a cuttingly satirical drawl.

'Oh, dear, I've upset you.' An understatement, she thought, regarding his taut expression with growing dismay. Well, at least there was no need to watch what she said any more—she had obviously talked herself out of a job.

Rafe brought his teeth together in a wolf-like smile. 'How long did you say you were married for?'

'I didn't, but it was two years.'

'*That* long?' he drawled insultingly.

'There's no need to be personal.' He released an incredulous laugh and she blushed. 'I'm just trying to say that a lot of men are…'

'Congenitally incapable of fidelity,' he finished smoothly. 'Whereas women never stray.'

'Of course they do.'

'Did you?'

'Chance would be a fine thing!' she snorted. 'When Mike walked out Rose was three months old.' As far as *straying* went, any idiot could figure out that this ruled out the twelve months prior to their separation. And afterwards, well… 'Would *you* want an affair with a woman who had a baby or young child?' she added cynically.

'Some people seem to be able to combine being a mother and lover…'

The fact he had avoided the question was not lost on Natalie. 'Whereas I can't even combine it with a career.'

Rafe released an exasperated sigh from between his clenched teeth. 'Self-pity doesn't suit you,' he observed drily. His brow creased. 'Wouldn't a nanny solve your problem? Or an au pair?'

Natalie gave an incredulous snort of laughter; nobody was that naïve, surely! She searched his face—he was serious! What world did this guy live in? Not one where you juggled half a dozen tasks simultaneously and did your supermarket shopping with a fretful child dragging along at your side.

No, Rafe lived in the glamorous world of the élite, flash cars, and flashier women, film premières and weekend skiing trips. It was hardly surprising that it was his world that sold newspapers and magazines to people whose own lives, like her own, were humdrum by comparison.

'Oh!' she cried, lifting a hand to her brow. 'Why didn't *I* think of that?' Her eyes narrowed. 'Maybe,' she added crisply, 'because I couldn't afford to pay for a full-time live-in nanny or even half a full-time nanny,' she added thoughtfully. 'The fact is you have it in for me,' she spelt out before he had a chance to respond, 'because I had the temerity to turn down that job offer!'

'*Have it in for you?*' he echoed incredulously. His narrowed eyes homed in on the accusing finger she was waving in front of his nose and with a grunt of sheer exasperation he caught the offending digit and, folding it into her palm, covered her small fist firmly with his own. Her hand was lost within his.

His grasp was firm but not constricting; Natalie could have pulled away, but she didn't. The blood drained from her face as, almost fearfully, she stared at the long, elegant fingers that looked very dark curled against her fair skin. Illogically the contrast excited her…a furtive excitement that she dared not admit even to herself.

His thumb began to move against the blue-veined inner aspect of her wrist and she let out a sharp gasp. A heat that began low in her belly suddenly flared hot and spread through her body invading every cell with a strange, enervating weakness. She raised her shocked eyes and Rafe smiled, a smile that held a terrifying mixture of sexual speculation and understanding as if he knew exactly how she was feeling. *Well, at least one of us does.*

'I was meant to be overcome with gratitude—' Natalie could barely hear her own hoarse whisper above the heavy throbbing beat of her heart.

'*Gratitude…? You…?*' he interjected with a wry laugh. 'I'm not *that* unrealistic.'

She continued as though he hadn't spoken. 'And I said no.' His skin was cool against her overheated flesh and there was controlled strength in his light touch that she found deeply exciting. 'You took it as a personal insult, that's why I've been given every crummy job going!' The moment the words were out of her mouth she wished them unsaid.

Determined not to lay herself open to an accusation of asking for preferential treatment, Natalie had consistently refused to complain…until now.

With an angry cry she wrenched her fingers away from his grasp and, covering them with her uncontaminated hand, nursed them against her chest.

'*Personal…!*' A feral smile illuminated the darkness of his face. He could have told her about personal—personal was wanting to take her face between his hands before kissing her senseless, the kind of kiss that might go some way to relieve a little of the frustration being around her filled him with. The errant nerve in his lean cheek began to pulse erratically as he visualised the pleasure of her willingly opening her lips to offer his tongue access to the soft sweetness of her mouth. His body reacted to the erotic imagery that filled his mind with all the subtlety and control of an adolescent boy.

Natalie was almost relieved when he frowned and suddenly barked, 'And what do you mean every crummy job going?' For a moment there the way he was looking at her had been almost frightening—not that she could ever have been *physically* scared of him, but there had been a combustible quality to his fixed stare that had been deeply unsettling.

By way of reply Natalie picked up a pile of documents from her desk and held them out to him. 'The perfect cure for insomnia,' she promised him.

'I don't suffer from it,' Rafael replied as he took them from her. He didn't look at them or—much to her relief—appear to notice when she snatched her hand away as if scalded when their fingertips accidentally brushed. 'I'm sorry if you feel your talents are being underused,' he replied, replacing the stack on her desk. He was detecting Maggie's handiwork here.

'Do you think I have any?' she exclaimed in mock amazement.

'You have a remarkable talent for making me lose my temper,' he told her drily. 'As for personal, you underestimate my ego…I have it on excellent authority that it is Teflon-coated.' The memory was one that seemed to entertain him—at least his expression had lost some of the edginess of a few moments ago that had made her feel uneasy. 'Apparently nothing short of a nuclear explosion could dent it.'

Natalie would have liked to meet the person who was daring and perceptive enough to tell him this to his face.

'My mother.'

Natalie's eyelashes swept down as she averted her gaze from his face; either she was awfully obvious or he was scarily perceptive. With my luck probably both, she concluded wryly.

'I hate to disappoint you, Natalie, but my job is to look at the big picture. I have neither the time or the inclination to exact revenge upon some junior members of staff with a lack of ambition.'

Well, that puts me firmly in my place, she thought bleakly. This seemed as good a time as any to remind herself that her position in the scheme of things at least at Ransome was a small and insignificant cog.

'I have ambition,' pride made her insist stubbornly. She lowered her eyes. 'But I also have other responsibilities,' she admitted with a rush. Her head came up. 'But that doesn't mean I'm asking for any special favours.'

'Why not?'

Natalie was perplexed by his unexpected response. 'Oh, sure, you're really geared up to parents…'

Rafe inhaled sharply and his hard-boned face darkened with annoyance. 'I don't think it's unreasonable to expect the people I employ to be capable of sorting out their personal lives without my unwanted interference, but that doesn't mean I'm unsympathetic when there's a problem.'

'I don't think anyone would want to invite you home to tea…' If they were talking beds she might be on shaky ground. The thought of the female staff who lusted after their good-looking boss brought a disgruntled frown to her smooth brow. 'But something as basic as a crèche and more flexible working hours might be appreciated.'

If she ever heard Mandy, his PA's scheme for a back-to-work package for new mums that included a voucher for a health spa he was in serious trouble! 'And you, I suppose, have been nominated to speak on behalf of this dissatisfied section of the workforce?' he interrupted smoothly.

'Not exactly,' she conceded, shifting her weight from one foot to the other under his ironic gaze. Not only did he make her feel like a gauche schoolgirl, now she was acting like one, too, she thought, only just stopping herself before she began to chew on a loose strand of hair—she hadn't done that since she was twelve, but at twelve she hadn't needed to distract herself from tender breasts that ached and tingled as they chafed against the fabric of her thin top.

Her chin lifted. 'A happier workforce makes for a more productive workforce…' she began defensively.

'Well, that's just fascinating. Have you any other little gems of management theory you'd like to share…any other little pearls of wisdom? You know I really ought to introduce you to the guy who drove me to the airport last week—he had some great ideas about how to run the country.'

CHAPTER FOUR

WHY am I even trying? Natalie wondered. The man is never
going to take advice from anyone, least of all me. Hell, he made
it pretty clear that I'm too low down the pecking order to even
approach him directly!

Even now the memory of Rafe's bored, 'Send my PA a
memo, Ms Warner,' had the power to send a flush of mortification over her skin. It had been especially hurtful because
before that he had seemed perfectly happy when she'd approached him; in fact she had found herself looking forward to
their conversations as the highlights of her days.

She had been deluded enough to think they'd been friends,
and had even—God, she cringed to think about it now!—spun
romantic little fantasies about them being more. That was why
him cutting her dead publicly had hurt so much. Since then she
had always been guarded and circumspect in front of him…until
today!

People had been very sympathetic, assuring her they'd never
seen him act like that before; the popular theory was he must
have been crossed in love. This explanation didn't seem at all
likely to Natalie as he seemed to change the women in his life
almost as frequently as he did his shirts and, as far as she could
tell, with about the same degree of emotional attachment.

'There's no need to be so damned patronising!' she exploded.
'I don't suppose it's your fault,' she added bitterly. 'It's probably
genetic.' The same genes that had made him the most physically
perfect specimen of manhood imaginable had also made him an
élitist sod. 'God, I bet you hate children!' sheer frustration made
her accuse wildly.

'Genetically impossible. My mother is Venetian and the—'

'I know your mother is Italian!' she snapped. '*Everybody*
knows that,' she added quickly—the last thing she wanted was

126

him to run away with the idea she took a personal interest in him. 'You're *famous*.'

Rafe had heard people say serial killer with the same distaste Natalie Warner managed to inject in 'famous'.

'My mother's family come from Venice. I make the distinction because she likes to—it's a regional pride thing. As I was about to say, the Italians adore children. I have a nephew and several godchildren...'

'And you think that makes you an expert?' Natalie laughed, blinking to clear her head of the image of Rafe with a golden-skinned baby in his arms...the irony was she had no doubt Rafe would be as exceptional at fatherhood as he was at everything else. In short, he'd be the sort of dad that Rose would never have. The thought brought an uneasy mixture of guilt, sadness and envy—*envy*...? Her smooth brow wrinkled as alarm shot through her. 'You'll find being a parent is quite different,' she told him with a superior sniff.

'I have no plans to find out any time soon, but you may be sure that when I do have a child I will be financially able to support a family and in a stable relationship.'

'Unlike me, you mean.'

'I have no idea of your personal circumstances.' Except that most of the unmarried men in the building would like to change them—and a number of the married ones, too, he thought grimly.

Natalie smiled. 'True, but don't let that stop you making judgement calls, will you?' Dark colour appeared across the crest of his sharply defined cheekbones; she was pleased to see that her jibe had found its mark.

'A child needs two parents.'

Natalie released an incredulous laugh...he thinks *I* need telling this? 'Did you read that somewhere or is this original thought we are hearing?' She shook her head in disgust. 'And what will you do if the other half of this *stable* relationship decides that she isn't ready after all for parenthood...or, for that matter, marriage? What if she packs her bags and says she has to leave because living with you is stifling h...her artistic creativity? That ...she doesn't love you any more and thinks maybe he never did!'

Natalie froze in horror as the lengthening silence continued to echo with the acrid bitterness of her last throbbing announcement. She was totally aghast at what she had said.

Why not just strip your soul bare, Natalie? Oh, I forgot, you already did! Her head sank to her chest as she closed her eyes. She couldn't bear to see what he was going to make of that. Her performance amounted to handing your enemy a loaded gun. *Rafe being the enemy and this being war?*

War…? The analogy struck her immediately as being on the extreme side. Why when Rafe was involved did she lose all sense of proportion—why did she go off the deep end so dramatically? Was this just a clash of personalities or was it a symptom of something much worse?

'I think I would consider myself well rid of such an idiot.'

Natalie was startled by this objective pronouncement, and her troubled gaze fluttered to his face. The bad news was he had seen through her hypothetical scenario; the good news was that nothing resembled the 'pity poor dumped wife' expression she hated so much in his face.

She gave a sigh—under the circumstances there didn't seem much point continuing the pretence. 'It wasn't really Mike's fault,' she protested. 'We were too young, and before we got married him being an artist unwilling to sacrifice his artistic integrity seemed quite romantic.' It had seemed a lot less desirable when they'd had rent to pay.

A spasm of distaste contorted Rafael's austerely handsome features—in his eyes a man who deserted a wife and young child was the lowest of the low.

'My God, I never took you for one of those pathetic females who defend the shiftless bastards who abuse and leave them!'

The lashing virulence of the anger in his voice took her aback almost as much as his accusation. It seemed she wasn't the only one in danger of going off the deep end.

'Mike wasn't abusive!' she protested. Her slender shoulders lifted. 'Just immature,' she judged generously.

Rafael raked a hand through his dark hair and gave vent to his feelings in a flood of musical Italian. It was the first time she had heard him revert to his mother's native tongue and, even though she doubted if the passionate invective translated into anything she'd like to hear, Natalie was spellbound.

Italian was not only beautiful to listen to, it was a very passionate language, she thought as his words flowed over her, smooth as warm honey. Did people who were bilingual find one language more appropriate than another for different activities...say English was good for booking theatre seats and Italian might be better for, say, making love?

'And I'm not pathetic,' she asserted, her voice rising to a panicky pitch as she tried to dispel from her head the shocking image of pale limbs entwined with dark gold. She closed her eyes in disgust and opened them with a snap when she felt the light touch of his fingers slide over the curve of her jaw. Her startled gaze collided head-on with burning blue eyes.

Natalie was too shocked by the casual physical contact to do anything but stare wide-eyed back at him like a night creature caught in the glare of headlights—and any headlights paled into insignificance beside his compelling cerulean gaze. There was no respite, no place to hide from the raking scrutiny of his lustrously lashed eyes.

Her lashes fluttered as the corners of his sternly beautiful mouth lifted; the action lessened the severity of his expression quite dramatically. His smile could have melted stone and Natalie's heart was not made of stone, and, though she liked to pretend otherwise, neither was it immune to this man's charismatic charm.

'No, not pathetic.' The half-smile reached his eyes and Natalie felt bathed in the warm glow of his approval...this was ridiculous!

It's not as if I care what he thinks of me! she thought. Care or not, she was mightily relieved when his hand fell back to his side. Are you so sure about that, Nat? Isn't there some secret part of you that wanted to prolong the contact...?

Rafe saw the tiny negative shake of her head and raised an interrogative brow.

The fight abruptly drained out of Natalie, leaving her feeling too weary to sustain her anger or resistance—Rafe was the most exhausting man to be around for any period of time. Or for that matter to be around period!

'Oh, for God's sake, if you're going to sack me or something get on with it.' She sighed, wearily sinking back into her chair.

She would have spun away from him but Rafe caught the back of her chair and turned it back towards him. Hands on the arm rests, his body curved over hers, he was an extremely big, powerful man and the action could have been intimidating, but it wasn't—it was exciting.

Natalie pressed a nervous hand to her neck. She could feel the dull vibration of her heartbeat in the hollow at the base of her throat. She was discovering that underneath his northern Celtic cool Rafe Ransome had inherited more of his mother's volatile Latin temperament than she had suspected. She might have been able to predict what Rafe would do in a given situation, but not *Rafael*, and the man who towered above her looked all Rafael.

'Or something.'

Natalie, who had forgotten what she'd said, didn't respond to the husky murmur. He was so close now that she could see the fine lines radiating from the corners of his eyes and the gold tips on the ends of his long sooty eyelashes. Through the dark concealing mesh she could see the shimmering summer-blue of his eyes. The tension in the air was so pronounced that she could almost see the invisible barrier that stood between them.

He appeared to be breathing hard; she could hear the soft, sibilant hiss of each inhalation and feel the intimate warmth of his breath whisper along her forehead and across the curve of her cheek. She found herself wondering what the texture of the dark shadow that emphasised the hollows of his cheeks and ran along his angular jaw would feel like if she ran her fingers over it... The achy, empty feeling low in her belly intensified as, unable to trust herself, she locked her fingers together tightly to prevent them doing something she'd regret.

He had angled his dark head so that the fragrant warmth now fell directly against her parted lips. The possibility he was going to kiss her no longer seemed so remote. Dizzy with anticipation, Natalie stopped breathing and closed her eyes.

It seemed like a long time later that his lips finally brushed against hers; Natalie's body stiffened, then relaxed. The pressure was light. It wasn't a lightness that could in any way have been construed as accidental; this was a leave-you-wanting-more, mind-blowingly erotic lightness.

And his technique worked. It worked like a dream. Maybe it was a dream…that was the only place she'd been kissed in a long time. She half wished it were a dream; people could behave irresponsibly in dreams and there were no consequences.

If this is a dream, don't let me wake up just yet.

'You're going to hate me in the morning,' he predicted throatily as his mouth moved with tantalising slowness down the slender curve of her throat.

'I already do,' she rebutted huskily.

'How much?' he asked, kissing her closed eyelids.

'You talk too much,' she complained.

Rafe laughed huskily, but there was nothing amused about his taut, driven expression. She looked into his smoky eyes and whimpered as his teeth gently tugged at the soft flesh of her lower lip. She bit him back and felt the purr of husky laughter in his throat.

'And there isn't going to be a night before to regret.' There wasn't; she was going to put a stop to this any minute now…any minute…

Well, what harm could another couple of minutes do? she told herself as she felt the pressure of his skilful lips subtly increase. It was just kissing.

Releasing a long, shuddering sigh, she ignored the alarmist voice of caution in her head that was insultingly suggesting she couldn't stop even if she wanted to, and instead responded to an instinct that impelled her to clutch at him to intensify and prolong the delicious experience. Weaving her fingers into his lush dark hair once she had done so seemed equally instinctual and very satisfying. If this went on for ever it wouldn't be too long, the dreamy thought drifted through her mind, before she gave herself up totally to the hedonistic pleasure of feeling his hard, rampantly male body pressed up against her.

Natalie hadn't known that kisses so addictive you couldn't walk away from them existed. Totally submerged by a tide of longing, she hooked her arms tightly around his neck. Rafe responded by encircling her narrow waist with his hands. With effortless ease he drew her upright, causing the chair he lifted her from to spin backwards until it collided noisily and unobserved into a filing cabinet.

Natalie wasn't even conscious that her shoes had slipped off as her toes lost contact with the floor.

'What if someone comes in…?'

Her agonised whisper caused him to pull back slightly. The flicker of cold reason in the passion-darkened eyes that swept over her flushed face brought the stupidity of what she was doing crashing home.

Her cheeks heated with mortification. 'This is really stupid.' She shook her head. 'We shouldn't be doing this.'

Rafe let his head fall back and she heard him exhale noisily. 'Sure,' he agreed, lifting his head and pinning her with a feverish cerulean stare. 'But think,' he advised her throatily, 'of the alternative.'

Natalie blinked in confusion.

'*Not* doing it.'

'*Oh!*' Every cell in her body screamed in protest.

'Precisely.'

Natalie was transfixed by the dark need stamped on his hard features.

'That would be…?'

His eyes slid to her mouth, then back to her eyes. 'Unthinkable,' he completed. Still holding her eyes, he parted her lips once more and with seductive skill slid his tongue between her trembling lips.

'Yes!' she whimpered, giving herself up to the craving she could no longer pretend didn't exist. '*Oh, yes, please!*'

Her fractured sob ached with longing. It was too much for Rafe's iron self-control, self-control she naïvely hadn't been aware existed until it was no longer there. A shudder rippled through his lean, powerful body the moment before he claimed her lips. His hungry lips had barely covered hers before his tongue stabbed deep again and again into her mouth.

Natalie was swept up into a maelstrom of pure sensation.

CHAPTER FIVE

NATALIE felt bereft and dizzy when Rafe abruptly put her from him.

'The phone is ringing.'

There was not a trace of the raw, driven hunger he had been exhibiting moments before in the hard planes and hollows of his face.

Natalie shivered, she suddenly felt very cold. He was going to pretend it hadn't happened... That was good, that was excellent—well, as excellent anything connected with kissing your boss with all the finesse of a sex-starved bimbo could be!

Just why had kissing him seemed a good idea? When she thought about how she had... Don't think about it, she instructed herself firmly. It didn't happen. If it works for him it works for me, she told herself angrily. It's just easier for him, she thought, sliding a resentful sideways glance at his darkly impassive face.

Rafe intercepted the look and exhaled loudly. 'This,' he grated, raking a hand through his hair in an exasperated manner, 'is *exactly* what I've been trying to avoid. Getting involved emotionally at work is a recipe for disaster.'

Wasn't that just typical of the man, acting as if he were the innocent victim of her shameless lust when he was the one who had started it? And that in itself was confusing. Why would a man who had spent the previous few minutes pulling all aspects of her appearance and character to shreds want to kiss her? Well, whatever the reason she wasn't going to accept all the blame.

'Afraid it wouldn't be good for your reputation if it got around you'd kissed someone with an inside-leg measurement of less than thirty-four?'

Initially Rafe looked startled by her caustic taunt, but within a matter of seconds an amused glint she didn't like appeared in his eyes.

'Or are you worried I'll play the sexual harassment card?

Don't be!' she advised, determined he would not be left with
the impression she envied in any way those blonde clones. Her
small bosom heaved as she sought to control her strong feelings.
'Do you think I *want* people to know you kissed me?' She gave
a very expressive little shudder.

'It's not *my* reputation I'm concerned about.'

'What are you talking about?'

'Have you any idea what people think about ambitious young
women who sleep with their bosses?' He paused to let his point
sink in. 'It doesn't matter how talented you happen to be, people
will always assume that you slept your way to the top.'

Natalie flushed. 'Some place I'm not likely to get!' she gritted.

'If you stop bleating and start actually being positive, it's not
totally impossible,' he declared callously.

Natalie glared at him with loathing.

'The phone is ringing again.'

'I know the phone is ringing, I don't need you to tell me,'
she snapped back childishly. 'Hello!' she snarled down the line.

'Is that you, Nat?' a puzzled voice the other end asked
tentatively.

It was hardly surprising, Natalie reflected grimly, that she
didn't sound like herself—she certainly didn't feel like herself!
And as for the way she'd been acting! How could you loathe
someone and want to rip their clothes off at the same time? She
turned her back on the tall, silent figure but it didn't stop her
being painfully aware of him in every cell of her body.

'Natalie?'

'Yes, it's me,' Natalie replied, recognising the familiar voice
of Ruth the child-minder. Alarm bells began to ring in her
head—Ruth never rang her at work unless there had been a
disaster of some sort. The last time Rose had been inconsolable
because she had lost her favourite teddy.

'Don't panic, Nat.'

Nothing, in Natalie's experience, was *less* likely to soothe
than a telephone conversation that began with these words, but
this was especially true if they were closely followed by a hor-
rifying, 'I'm ringing from the hospital.'

Not a lost teddy this time.

This was the sort of phone call that every parent dreaded getting. An icy fist of frozen fear closed around Natalie's heart as a dozen scenarios, each one more catastrophic than the one preceding it, chased rapidly through her head. The panic racing through her veins made it hard for her to think straight. Her lips felt stiff and reluctant to form the question she knew she had to ask, but desperately didn't want to.

'Is she...?'

There was a gasp the other end. 'Oh, God, no, Rose is fine!' The child-minder sounded horrified. 'Well, not *fine*, obviously, or we wouldn't be here, but she will be, they say.'

Natalie's shoulders sagged. *'Oh, my God!'* She was not conscious of Rafe retrieving her chair and sliding it behind her knees at the crucial moment they gave way.

A strange numbness spread through her body while in her head she could feel the dull throb of her own heartbeat.

'After you left Rose seemed a bit feverish,' Ruth relayed hurriedly. 'And later when she started wheezing the inhaler didn't work. I thought the best thing was to get her here first and then ring you.'

'You did the right thing, Ruth.' Natalie caught her trembling lower lip in her teeth. 'I should have listened to my instincts,' she gulped. 'Oh, God, I knew, I just *knew* I shouldn't have left her...but the doctor said she was fine this morning, just a cold...' She stopped, her expression one of grim self-condemnation. She couldn't pass the buck. Nobody had forced her to come into work; that had been her own decision. Because I have a point to prove—namely that a single parent can be just as good...no, *better* than everyone else.

And while I was busy proving my point my daughter was... She shook her head in disgust. What sort of parent does that make me?

Ruth's sensible voice injected a note of practicality into the endless flow of bitter self-recriminations.

'Natalie, dear, if you listened to your instincts you'd never leave Rose at all.'

'Maybe that isn't such a bad idea,' Natalie replied heavily. 'Listen, tell her Mummy will be there soon...yes...all right,

Ruth, and thank you,' she said, placing the receiver down and rising urgently to her feet.

Her eyes drifted over him, but from the vague, unfocused expression in them Rafe doubted she had even registered his presence.

He watched as she opened her handbag and, extracting a wallet from the depths, began flicking through the contents with an expression of fierce concentration on her pale features. Her hands were trembling but he doubted she was aware of it; she was displaying all the classic symptoms of shock.

'Where are you going, Natalie?'

Natalie swung back and as she saw him standing there Rafe saw a flicker of shock replace for a moment the fretful expression in her wide, darkly lashed eyes—clearly she had forgotten he was there. This female, he thought wryly, seemed to be determined to single-handedly supply the dose of humility his mother—not a person exactly renown for modesty herself—liked to say he needed so badly.

'You called me Natalie,' she heard herself say stupidly.

'It's your name,' he reminded her gently.

'It sounds…different when you say it,' she observed in a distracted voice. 'My daughter is in hospital.' She looked around the familiar room as if she was surprised to find herself still there. 'I have to go…' She glanced briefly towards the mess on her desk and then back at him. '*Now,*' she added, dealing him a ferocious frown.

Clearly she thought he was an inconsiderate louse who would demand she cleared her desk before she went to her sick child, which was a great basis for a relationship. *Relationship…?* First you break the 'mixing business with pleasure' rule, which is bad, but not as bad as wanting to break it some more. Now you're thinking *relationships*! he derided himself. What next…?

'Which hospital is she in?'

Natalie told him because it was easier than telling him to mind his own business and because he was blocking her way. Actually his calm voice helped her focus her thoughts. Rafe was the sort of man that women less able than herself to take care of themselves would have automatically leaned on in a situation like this.

Natalie was fully awake to the pitfalls of leaning on a man...when they walked away you either fell flat on your face or learnt how to do things for yourself. Of course, Mike had never exactly been a pillar of strength to begin with, so it hadn't been so difficult for her. In fact the gap he'd left in her life had been pretty insignificant all things considered... Rafe Ransome, on the other hand—her wary glance flickered to his tall, vital person—well, nothing about him was insignificant!

'Give me a minute and I'll take you.'

Natalie stared at him incredulously. *'You?'*

'It's on my way.'

She looked up at him, a sceptical line between her dark, feathery brows, clearly trying to figure out his ulterior motive. He couldn't help her out; he still wasn't sure if he had one himself.

'On your way where?'

'I can give you a detailed run-down of my itinerary or I can take you to the hospital.' He gave a very Latin take-it-or-leave-it shrug. 'Unless you prefer to take your chance with public transport?'

Natalie's thoughts turned to the empty condition of her wallet. If anyone had asked her earlier that day she'd have stated with total confidence that nothing on earth would have persuaded her to accept a lift from Rafe Ransome...the man who had just kissed her—*and you kissed him back!*

If her lips hadn't still felt bruised and swollen she would have imagined it had been another of those erotic dreams that woke her up more nights than she cared to admit.

Impatiently she shook her head; she couldn't think about that now.

Swallowing her pride, she lifted her eyes to his. 'Thank you.' It wasn't, she told herself, as if she were sleeping with the enemy, just riding with him. 'Don't be long!' Her anxiety and impatience made the request emerge as an imperious command.

Rafe turned, looking about as surprised as it was possible for someone like him to look. It occurred to Natalie that he wasn't used to being on the receiving end of yelled orders. Not, she acknowledged, that he did any yelling—he didn't need to. He could silence any would-be dissident with a look.

'You did say you'd only be a minute,' she reminded him, moderating her tone. 'You might forget I'm here…' she added defensively.

For a brief moment his narrowed eyes scanned her face. 'I've already tried to do that…and failed,' he revealed cryptically. A rather grim smile lifted the corners of his mouth as she looked back at him warily. 'Don't worry, Natalie, I'm renowned for my attention to detail and timing.'

This time his grin was frankly wicked.

True to his word, he was back within the minute. He walked towards her, shrugging on a dark, loose-fitting suit jacket, and the expensive fabric fell smoothly into place across his broad back. That never happens to me, she thought as she fell in step beside him. She quickly got breathless trying to keep up with his long-legged pace.

'Is there anyone you want to contact…to meet you at the hospital…?' he probed when they reached the underground parking area.

'No.'

'A friend, relation…your daughter's father, perhaps?'

Natalie, her mind on more urgent matters, was exasperated by his persistence. 'My grandmother is my only relation and she lives in Yorkshire. Hospitals freak Mike out.'

And she couldn't cope with a man who went catatonic when he saw a white coat as well as a sick and almost certainly fretful child. Mike would appear when Rose was back home, bearing expensive and often inappropriate gifts. He meant well, she thought indulgently, now she didn't have to contend with her ex-husband's foibles on a daily basis.

Rafe was not inclined to be so generous. It seemed pretty obvious to him that there had been two children in her marriage. He found it inexplicable that women were frequently attracted to the inadequate types who traded on their boyish charm.

'And is your daughter…?'

Natalie's expression softened. 'Rose.'

'Is Rose ill often?'

'No more than a lot of children,' Natalie replied defensively. 'Well,' she conceded, her eyes falling self-consciously from his, 'I suppose she is. She's asthmatic. She's fine normally with the medication. Only winter's not a good time…a cold or virus can trigger a nasty attack in some sensitive people.'

'I've heard that pollution from exhaust fumes and so forth can make matters worse.'

His depth of knowledge surprised her. 'It doesn't help,' she agreed, nodding her thanks stiffly as he opened the passenger door of a black Jag. She slid inside the luxurious interior, her tense back remaining a good two inches clear of the backrest as Rafe belted himself into the driver's seat.

'Haven't you considered moving out of the city—if it would improve your daughter's health?'

Natalie tucked a strand of hair behind her ear and threw him an impatient look. 'Some of us have to live where the work is.' She gave a dry laugh. 'Always supposing I still have work. Does it feel good to hold my fate in your hands?'

Dark colour scored the slashing angles of his high cheekbones as he turned the key in the ignition. The powerful engine came to life. 'You've got me—we egomaniacs just love wielding power.' He turned his head and his dark lashes dipped as his glance moved with deliberation over the length of slender body. 'Only actually in this instance it felt even better to hold your body in my hands.' A firm, supple and surprisingly strong body that had proved amazingly responsive to his lightest touch.

For the briefest of moments their eyes collided. The anger in his made her recoil, but it wasn't the anger that made her look away, her heart thudding hard against her ribcage. The message in his smoky eyes had been explicitly sexual in nature…and worse was the fact her entire body responded to what she had seen.

God, she despaired, I am obviously a desperately shallow person and a terrible mother to boot to be feeling this way when my daughter is lying sick in hospital.

'I think we should discuss what happened back there…'

Natalie shook her head. 'As far as I'm concerned it didn't happen.' If she told herself this often enough, maybe she would even start believing it herself. She thought for a moment he was going to contest her statement, but after a brief nod in her direction he returned his attention to the road.

It had taken Rafe several frustrating minutes to find a parking space, so when he walked into the busy casualty department he had no expectation of finding Natalie still there.

She was.

He summed up the situation at one glance. Natalie was standing at the back of a queue several people deep that had built up behind an aggressively awkward drunk who was giving the young woman at the reception desk in the busy casualty department a hard time.

'I know my rights!' the dishevelled figure slurred loudly enough for Rafe and everyone around to hear.

Natalie, who was struggling to contain her impatience, heard the subdued murmurs of complaint as someone shouldered through the people who were waiting ahead of her, but didn't pay much attention. It wasn't until a few moments later when she glanced up that she recognised the tall, broad-shouldered figure. She cringed with embarrassment when she saw what he was doing!

Typical, she thought angrily. Rafael Ransome thinks he's too damned special to wait his turn. As she watched he began to speak in a low voice to the befuddled guy who had been holding everyone up. There was nothing threatening about his body language and the conversation, considering the older man's loud hostility, seemed to be perfectly amicable. Possibly too amicable for Rafe, she thought as the drunk suddenly threw his arms about the younger man's neck and announced to everyone that this was a good guy!

Natalie watched in disbelief as the man let Rafe lead him back to a seat in the waiting area and bring him a drink from the vending machine. It would seem that *nobody* was immune to Rafe's charm and persuasiveness.

By the time the overtaxed security team arrived the queue was moving smoothly and Rafe had, much to Natalie's discomfort, joined her.

'Did you have to interfere? What if he'd got nasty? You could have made things worse.' She heard her voice rise to an unattractive, shrill accusing note. 'You should have left it for the people who are paid to deal with that sort of thing,' she gritted. 'The ones who know what they're doing.'

One of that number chose that precise moment to approach them. 'Cheers, mate,' he said, slapping Rafe on the shoulder. 'Understand we owe you one. Old Charlie's a regular,' he explained, nodding in the direction of the old man who was now snoring happily away. 'But he can get nasty. Last time he took a swing at a nurse.'

'See, you shouldn't have interfered,' Natalie insisted, glaring up at the modest hero. 'Have-a-go heroes usually get themselves or someone else hurt.'

'Well, I didn't.'

Natalie, who was feeling physically ill visualising a scenario where he had got injured, didn't reply.

'I just need to find out which ward they've taken Rose to,' she explained hoarsely. 'You don't need to hang around,' she added pointedly.

Rafe smiled down into her face but didn't budge.

To Natalie's intense annoyance, when it was her turn and she enquired about Rose from the pretty girl behind the desk it was to Rafe the young woman replied.

'Your little girl has been taken up to Ward Six. If you and your wife—'

'She's not *his* little girl and *I* am not his wife!' Natalie snarled before she stamped away. 'That should make you happy,' she added under her breath. It just made her sick that some women were so *obvious*, and some men just lapped it up.

'You think I'm in with a chance there, then?'

He must have incredibly acute hearing. 'Listen, I'm grateful you got me here,' she said, sounding anything but, 'but, like I said, there's absolutely no need for you to stay.' As she spoke they came to another intersection; Natalie took the right turn without looking at the direction sign overhead.

'I take it you've been here before,' Rafe observed drily.

'Why *are* you still here?' she puffed, genuinely puzzled by his continued presence.

'It would be like walking out before the end of a film if I left now…I'd be wondering all night what happened.'

They had reached the door to the ward. Natalie pressed the buzzer and waited. Still slightly breathless from the brisk jogging pace he'd set, she tilted up her head to the man beside her—it went without saying that he wasn't out of breath. Just looking at him standing there in his designer suit with not a hair out of place made her bristle with antagonism. How had she ever imagined they could be friends…?

'I'm so glad we are providing some entertainment for you!' she exclaimed bitterly. 'Better than interactive telly.'

A muscle clenched in his lean cheek. 'For God's sake, woman, it was a joke. I know you think I'm some sort of heartless creep…' It was pretty hard to miss the fact—she didn't fall over herself to deny this estimation. 'What is it with you? Why can't you accept people want to help? Why do you throw their concern back in their faces?'

The anger faded from his face as he looked into her pale, upturned features—too-bright eyes looked back at him. He judged that she was keeping going on nervous tension alone. Take that away and she would shatter like a piece of the fragile porcelain she reminded him of.

Natalie blinked. '*You* want to help…?'

'I'd like to stay until you find out how your daughter is.' Rafe's frustrated urge to protect her from dead-beat ex-husbands and her own stubborn independence found release in a fresh burst of anger. 'You'll drive yourself into the ground with this I-don't-need-anyone stuff,' he predicted grimly. 'Who's going to look after your daughter then?' Natalie winced at this brutal observation. 'Your loser ex…?'

Her eyes filled with tears. Nice one, you always have to go too far, don't you, Rafe…?

'If you want me to go, just say so and I will,' he grunted.

Gold-shot green locked with electric-blue and Natalie's mind went a blank, then from out of nowhere she heard herself say, 'No! No, I don't want you to go.'

Natalie saw some emotion, strong but unidentifiable, flicker in the back of his eyes and she went pink. Her no hadn't been a laid-back, if-you-like sort of no, more a raw, you'll-leave-over-my-dead-body sort of no. Another of those silences filled with dangerous currents began to stretch between them. It was broken when a crackly voice emerged from the speaker on the wall.

With a sigh of relief Natalie identified herself and the door clicked open.

She turned to Rafe and gave an offhand shrug. 'I didn't mean to be rude but I'm used to doing this alone.'

'And do you like it that way?'

'I haven't had much choice. Someone has to make the decisions and I'm the one on the spot,' she explained matter-of-factly. 'You can stay if you like, but you'll have to wait here.' She nodded towards some seats and left him. She had no expectation that he would still be there when she returned.

He was.

CHAPTER SIX

NATALIE stopped mid-yawn and stared. 'You're still here!' The clock on the wall behind him read half-past midnight.

Rafe languidly uncurled his long, lean length from the uncomfortable-looking chair that was far too small to accommodate him and stretched. The action caused his shirt to pull tight, revealing the definition of his well-developed chest muscles shadowed by dark body hair and his washboard-flat belly.

She knew she was staring but tiredness made Natalie less able to adequately disguise the effect this disturbing spectacle was having on her—if not from him, certainly from herself. Finally in a position where she couldn't hide from the truth, she could hardly believe that she'd been walking around for weeks acting as if the facts her blood pressure went rocketing and she couldn't think straight when he was around were simply a coincidence.

Talk about fooling yourself!

'Why...?' she asked, closing her eyes briefly while she regained a degree of composure. Now she had accepted how attracted to him she was, she could guard against it. If she'd been more honest sooner that kiss might not have happened.

When she opened her eyes again Rafe had fastened a button on his loose-fitting jacket. She watched, her expression carefully neutral, as he smoothed back his thick hair, which to her eyes seemed perfectly ordered. She found herself considering how it might feel to mess it up again...to run her fingers deep into that lush— *Stop that, Natalie!*

'I had nowhere else to be.'

Natalie could not allow a lie this blatant to pass unchallenged. 'I find that difficult to believe.'

'So now you're wondering what my ulterior motives are. Actually, Natalie...I fell asleep,' he ruefully revealed in the manner of someone making a clean breast of it. 'I had a long session with Magnus Macfaden today...the usual battle of attrition.'

He seemed genuine enough and she supposed the explanation was just about plausible.

'No wonder you're tired, then.' Natalie had never met the head of the famous electronics firm but she had heard about him. 'I'm just surprised you managed to sleep through the noise.' Everyone entering and leaving the ward would have passed by him and it had been a busy evening.

'Oh, I can sleep anywhere, any time.'

'And with whoever you want, but then you already know that. Everyone who reads a tabloid knows that.' *Please tell me I didn't just say that out loud.*

'Are your objections moral or personal?' he enquired with interest.

'Neither!' she squeaked. 'Your personal life is your own business.'

'It's not nearly as...*active*, as the papers would have you believe.'

'Whatever,' she said, evincing disinterest.

'How is your daughter?'

'Rose is much better, thanks. She's finally asleep and off the nebuliser. I just thought I'd stretch my legs; if you fall asleep in one of those chairs you can't move in the morning.'

Rafe let his head fall back and flexed his shoulders. 'That I can believe,' he grimaced.

'What you need is a massage,' she observed without thinking—at least, she was thinking, but of things she had no business to be thinking about.

A half-smile played around his lips. 'Are you offering...?'

Natalie went as red as it was possible to go without spontaneously combusting. *'Most certainly not!'*

His suggestive sigh of pity combined with the lingering image in her head of her hands sliding over oiled golden flesh made her stomach muscles flutter madly. Their eyes touched and the liquid heat pooled shockingly between her thighs.

'Have you done many all-night stints in the chairs?'

Natalie couldn't look at him.

'One or two. You know, about that kiss earlier...I don't want you to get the wrong idea...' she said awkwardly.

'What idea would that be?'

'I don't…well, I don't have casual relationships. It wouldn't be fair to Rose for her to get fond of a man only to have him disappear from her life. She's already had that happen once. I'm not saying this because I think you want to…'

'Yes, you do, and you're right.'

'You w…want me…?' Her cheeks burned. 'I mean you…'

'Right first time.' Natalie's jaw dropped. 'Listen, I hear what you're saying about your daughter, but what are you going to do, remain celibate?'

'It's worked for me so far.' She saw the flicker of shock in his eyes and hurried on. 'People put far too great an emphasis on sex.'

'It's a very basic need. Sex is like any other appetite…'

'For men maybe.'

'For women, too, trust me…' he drawled.

'Do I look that stupid?'

'A lot of women don't want a deep and meaningful relationship. A hotel room and a long lunch hour,' he elaborated crudely. 'Functional sex is more to their taste. Maybe you should try and develop a taste for that if you don't want any involvement.'

Was he trying to insult her? She found the idea of the sort of cold-blooded clinical encounter he described appalling. 'Is that what you're offering me?'

'I thought it was the other way around.' He didn't have the faintest idea why the idea of sex without the complications should outrage him so much.

'How do you figure that one?'

'Well, you do want to keep your home a male-free zone…'

'How does that put me in a hotel room with you?' Natalie tried to sound amused and failed.

'You don't *seriously* expect the attraction between us to simply go away, do you? Pretending it's not there doesn't work— we've tried that! It's inevitable that we'll end up in bed at some point.'

'How dare you talk to me like that?' she gasped.

'I dare because I'm the man who wants to go home with you,' he reminded her softly.

Natalie's eyes widened; this was news to her and, maybe from his expression, Rafe, too.

She bit her lip. 'We can't talk about this here.'

'Then I hope for the sake of my sanity that you're not going to be here long?'

'I think they're going to let us out in the morning this time,' she revealed, half of her wishing it were longer if it meant she didn't have to confront the issues he had raised. 'Which is a big relief. If Rose hadn't got to go to the wedding I don't like to think what sort of fuss she'd have kicked up.'

'*Wedding?*'

'Yes, the one that Luke was going to come to with me. Rose is going to be bridesmaid at her dad's wedding—on Valentine's Day,' she explained with a wry smile. Mike had not been such a romantic when he'd been married to her.

'You're going to your ex's wedding?'

Natalie grimaced at the incredulity in his voice; she'd seen that response before. 'Before you ask, I'm not actually a masochist, or that forgiving, it's just Rose wants me to come and see her in her bridesmaid dress, and Mike might not be my husband any more but he'll always be her father,' she explained gravely.

The last thing she wanted to become was one of those mothers who bad-mouthed their ex-partners to the kid caught in the middle.

Despite her apparent composure when she mentioned her ex, Rafael couldn't help but wonder if she had come to terms with the situation quite as well as she liked people to think. Inexplicably any number of women nurtured passions for men who treated them appallingly. He frowned as he scanned her face for signs of the secret passion he had half convinced himself she was nursing. It was quite possible Natalie still carried a torch for the pathetic jerk.

'And Luke was going with you?'

'He was,' she confided with a sleepy yawn.

'Then you two are...?'

'Just good friends. This is so strange...' she mused.

'What's so strange, Natalie?'

'Talking to a real person...as in one who is over ten,' she elaborated, 'here.' Her gesture took in the walls, which were covered in brightly coloured childish paintings. 'The nurses are lovely but they're always so busy.' She was totally unaware of the wistful note in her voice. 'And sometimes you just want to talk to someone who doesn't consider tomato ketchup on chips the height of sophistication.'

'I will try and do my best to supply some adult conversation.'

'So long as you remember that's *all* I want.'

'How could I forget? Why was Luke going with you?'

'If you must know, I didn't want to turn up alone looking like a sad loser.'

'Why would you look like a sad loser?'

Natalie threw him a pitying look—this man knew nothing about being a single female approaching thirty or, for that matter, looking like a sad loser. She was dimly aware that a combination of exhaustion and relief was making her not just light-headed, but dangerously garrulous, too.

'Think about it,' she suggested. 'I'm a woman whose husband left her for a gorgeous blonde and *everyone* knows a female is unfulfilled unless she is half of a partnership.'

'I hesitate as a mere man to disagree, but isn't that a slightly old-fashioned attitude?'

'It's the way it is. I suppose I should have the guts to be single and proud; asking Luke to pretend to be my lover is even more pathetic than being dumped. *Poor Luke.*'

'And I sent Luke away.'

Natalie nodded and took the cup of coffee he handed her from the vending machine. Nursing it, she sat down on one of the nasty, shiny fake leather seats. 'You could say you owe me a pretend lover.' She took a sip and winced as the scalding liquid burnt her tongue.

'Then I suppose I'm obligated to provide you with a substitute.'

'Know a good escort agency, do you? Mind you, even if you

did I doubt if I could afford the rates of the sort of place you would use.' She chuckled weakly at her joke.

Rafe blinked. 'I can't say anyone has ever accused me of being au fait with high-class escort services before.'

'Gracious, I didn't mean...I don't think that you...' She gave a gusty sigh of relief. 'You were winding me up? I thought you were about to sack me for sure, or have you already done that? I forget,' she admitted with a yawn.

'No, and I have a suggestion to put to you. I have this idea about starting up a facility to offer advice to small businesses...' He stopped. 'Well, like you said, this isn't the place and you are dead on your feet.'

'I'm fine.'

'Sure you are,' Rafe murmured as he took the seat beside hers.

'I'll just rest my eyes for a minute.'

'Good idea.'

The periods her lashes lay against her waxily pale cheek before she forced her eyes open got gradually longer. For some time after her head had fallen against his shoulder Rafe stayed still, afraid to wake her. When it became obvious nothing was going to do that he shifted so that he could look at her sleeping face. It was the sort of face a man could look at for a long time without growing tired—maybe never!

Natalie woke in a strange bed. It took a few panicky moments before she recognised her spartan surroundings. She wished she weren't so familiar with the small room reserved for parents who wanted to stay overnight with their children.

Yawning, she threw back the covers. She was still fully dressed. Her frown deepened as she saw her shoes neatly placed at the bedside. She couldn't recall putting them there or, for that matter, taking them off. In fact she had no recollection of getting into bed at all—the last thing she remembered was in fact... *Good God!*

She hadn't forgotten because she hadn't done any of those things, which meant that someone had done them for her. That meant...

The nurse at the desk looked up as Natalie approached.

'Oh, you're awake.' She smiled. 'I was just going to take your boyfriend a cup of tea. Would you like one?'

'My boyfriend?' Natalie echoed warily.

'He's in with Rose. He's got quite a way with her, hasn't he?' she observed. 'Until he turned up I thought we were going to have to wake you. She was really cranky when she woke.'

'Why didn't you wake me?'

'Your boyfriend said to let you sleep.'

'He did?'

'You must have been tired,' the nurse reflected, oblivious to the grim note in Natalie's voice. 'You didn't stir when he put you to bed,' she recalled.

Natalie gulped. 'Rafe put me to bed?' Rafe, it seemed, had been busy. Not content with deciding what was best for her, he was usurping her authority with her child as well! The man just couldn't help taking charge. Well, he was about to learn that she didn't need anyone to make her decisions. She chose to forget all the occasions when the burden of making all the decisions concerning Rose's welfare had lain heavily upon her shoulders.

'Carried you like a baby,' the youthful health professional confirmed with a very unprofessional gleam of envy in her eyes.

Natalie decided it was high time she put the record straight. 'He's not my boyfriend, he's my boss.'

'*Boss?*'

'Yes, boss,' Natalie declared defiantly as she stomped off.

Rose's bed was in a bay of four but at that moment she was the only occupant. Natalie's impetuous stride halted as she entered. The main lights in the ward were dimmed but the night light above Rose's bed illuminated the area beneath. And the people.

Rose was seated cross-legged on top of the duvet and Rafe sat in an easy chair, leaning on the bed with his dark head resting on his crossed arms. She could not see his face but she could hear the deep rumble of his voice in the quiet of the room. Rose too was listening to what he was saying, her little face rapt.

An emotional lump formed in Natalie's throat as she stared at the tableau. She'd never been more aware of the things that, even with the best will in the world, she couldn't provide in Rose's life.

Suddenly Rose's childish laughter rang out and, brushing the back of her hand across the dampness on her cheeks, Natalie moved forward to reveal herself.

'Mummy, Rafe's been telling me a story about a boy who had a pet dragon but nobody else can see him.'

'Mr Ransome has been very kind, but he's got to go now and you must get some sleep, so snuggle down.'

Reluctantly the child complied. 'Kiss,' she commanded imperiously to Rafe, who complied.

'Well what have I done now?'

Natalie pulled a concealing curtain around them. 'Where to start?' she hissed. 'How about with taking unilateral decisions?'

'You needed the sleep, Natalie.'

'I need to stay in control. Listen, you've been very kind, but—'

'Butt out and clear off. Right, am I allowed to say goodbye to Rose?'

'Of course.' His swift surrender had deflated her.

'I'll see you on the fourteenth?' The curtain rattled as he pulled it aside.

Natalie frowned. *'Fourteenth?'*

The wedding.

'We agreed it was the least I could do as I had robbed you of Luke.'

'I didn't agree to anything...' Natalie's brow furrowed as she tried to think back, but her recollections were frustratingly hazy. *'Did I...?'*

Rafe smiled. 'Morning dress, right? Oh—' he turned back '—don't even *think* about coming into work tomorrow or Friday. No buts, *I'm* the one in control there.' Or so goes the rumour, he added drily to himself as he walked away.

CHAPTER SEVEN

'OH, YES, very nice,' Mike said vaguely as his daughter waved her new patent leather shoes in his face for his approval. Deliberately not looking at his ex-wife's angry white face, he bent down awkwardly to his daughter's level. 'How would you like to come with me and Gabby to America, Rosie?' he asked the excited child in a coaxing voice.

'Will I see dolphins?'

Mike, who didn't have the faintest idea that his little daughter was fascinated by dolphins, looked momentarily nonplussed by this response. 'Sure we'll see dolphins.'

'Will Mummy be coming?'

'No.'

The child's face fell. 'Well, thank you very much,' she said politely, 'but I think I'll stay at home.'

Mike's smile grew fixed. 'In America we'll have a swimming pool in the garden.'

Rose's eyes grew round. *In the garden!* she gasped in awe. 'We don't have a garden here, but we have a window-box.'

Natalie gritted her teeth as Mike shot her a triumphant look and hissed, 'Out of the mouth of babes.'

'Rose, go and put on those pretty socks we bought to go with your dress and then you can go with Daddy to have the man put flowers in your hair.'

'Why can't you do that?'

'Because Aunt Gabby's friend is much better at fixing flowers in your hair than I am.' He'd have to be, she reflected grimly, to justify the expense of Gabby flying him along with a make-up artist across the Atlantic to fix the bridal parties' hair and faces.

Ironically, when Mike had turned up in person to take his daughter to the hotel suite where Gabby and the other brides-

152

maids had spent the night she had actually felt touched by the gesture. *How naïve does that make me?*

She waited until the little girl had danced away before turning furiously to her ex-husband. Without preamble she grabbed him by the lapel of his morning suit—that got his attention.

'Good God, Natalie, there's no need to get physical!'

'That just about sums up our marriage.'

Mike coloured. 'What's got into you, Natalie?'

'You can ask that? You come here on the *morning* of your wedding,' she began in a quivering voice of disbelief, 'to tell me you're going to apply for full custody of Rose. What do you think has *got into me*? You must be insane if you think I'm going to allow you and Gabby to take Rose out of the country!' she hissed. 'Besides, no court in the country would give you custody just because Gabby doesn't want to risk stretch marks,' she mocked, releasing him and pressing a hand to her trembling lips.

Was there…?

Mike looked shaken but stubbornly determined as he smoothed the fabric she had released. 'Our lawyer doesn't agree with you, Nat. He says we have a very good chance. What can you offer Rose compared with us?' He looked around the neat little room with distaste.

'*Love…?*' Natalie suggested ironically.

'Sure, sure, we all love Rosie, she's a cute kid.'

'And she's house-trained.'

'It's the quality of life we can give her,' Mike insisted piously. 'She needs a proper family life.'

'Pity, you didn't seem to think so when you walked out on us.'

Mike flushed angrily. 'You're a single parent, Nat, living in a poky little flat. You're always saying how you struggle to make ends meet.'

'That could have something to do with the twelve months you didn't pay me child support.'

'Yes, well, things have changed. Since the exhibition I'm doing very well and, besides, I'd have thought you'd have been grateful to have someone else take the burden off your shoulders.'

'Rose is not a burden and if you ever say that in front of her I'll make sure you regret it.'

'For God's sake, Nat, what do you take me for?'

'A selfish, insensitive prat…shall I go on?'

'There's no need to get abusive. With us Rosie would have all the advantages and opportunities money can buy.'

'Money can't buy everything.' It could buy lawyers, though; lawyers who could twist the facts to suit their clients.

'*And* we're a married couple.'

Natalie felt a fresh flurry of uncertainty. He might be bluffing, but then again perhaps such things did still weigh heavily? 'Nobody cares about that sort of thing…?'

Mike heard the uncertainty in her voice and smiled. 'I know this is hard for you—' he placed a hand on her shoulder '—but you have to think about what is best for Rosie, Nat.'

Eyes flashing fire, Natalie angrily shrugged off his hand.

'Am I early?'

The couple, who had been too engrossed in their argument to hear the approach of the new arrival, turned towards the figure in the open doorway.

'And who the hell are you?' Mike demanded.

Rafe unhurriedly transferred his attention from Natalie's tense face. He did not feel very well disposed towards the man who had put that shadowed look of distress in her eyes and he saw no reason to disguise the fact.

'I'm Rafael Ransome,' Rafe announced, giving himself his full title. 'And you,' he observed, managing without changing expression to convey that he wasn't overly impressed with what he was seeing, 'must be the bridegroom.'

Natalie, who had never seen Rafe conduct himself with this particular brand of chilling hauteur before, wasn't surprised that Mike looked uncomfortable and angry to be on the receiving end of such studied insolence.

Identification established, Rafe seemed to lose interest in the other man almost immediately. He turned to Natalie, the warmth in his eyes a stark contrast to the dismissive contempt of moments before. He opened his hand and revealed a bunch of keys before placing them beside a colourful pot plant on a leather-banded ship's chest that had been a junk-shop find.

'I thought I'd lost them!'

Before Rafe had arrived she'd thought that Mike looked pretty impressive in his expensive morning suit and handmade shoes. Now that he stood beside Rafe she could see that she had been mistaken. Even if they had been dressed by the same tailor Mike would always have looked like a pale imitation standing next to this extraordinary man.

It wasn't just the fact that Rafe had a body that was better than incredible—anyone with enough discipline could achieve a six pack, she thought, eyeing his flat belly and feeling her own stomach muscles tighten. No, what made Rafe was that extra special ingredient that separated the leader of the pack from the common herd. He didn't have to try, he just had...well... *presence*.

Worriedly, she examined her reaction when she'd seen him standing there. Casting herself on her boss's broad chest every time he appeared was not the best way to hide the fact you were having an affair with him—or were about to. She wondered what Rafe would say if he knew that she had decided to...to...sleep with him. Hell, I can hardly think it, let alone say it. Do I have a problem!

Of course you have a problem—you're in love with the man. You could only ignore something that was staring you in the face for just so long.

'You should be more careful with your keys,' he chided.

Natalie gulped and nodded. Oh, God, you don't know the half of it! Sure, he wanted an affair, he'd made that plain, but a clingy woman who wanted to offer him her heart—that really wasn't Rafe's style.

Mike, who had been watching this interchange with a sour expression, cleared his throat.

'Listen, if you don't mind, Nat and I were having a *private* conversation.' His hostility was still there, but it was not so overt now he had had the opportunity to fully take in the size and quality of the new arrival.

Rafe didn't even look at the other man; his steady gaze remained fixed on Natalie's face. 'Do you want me to go, Natalie?' In contrast to the intense expression in his eyes, his tone was light.

Natalie took a deep breath and turned to face her ex-husband. 'I don't have any secrets from Rafe,' she claimed.

Mike frowned. 'Since when?'

Probably something Rafe himself was wondering, too. Natalie didn't dare check out his reaction, sure that if she did her resolve would fail. She took a deep breath and plunged recklessly onwards.

'Since we decided to get married,' she announced casually.

A stunned silence followed her words.

'Well, now, isn't that convenient?' Mike drawled, quite obviously, despite his amused tone, thrown by her declaration.

Natalie was excruciatingly aware of the still, silent presence of the man beside her; she could only imagine how shocked Rafe had been to hear he was going to get married. She turned warily to look at him; with one word he could blow her out of the water. She had no way of knowing from his expression if the silent message she was desperately trying to telegraph him had been received.

'Not had time to buy a ring yet, then?'

Natalie flushed and tucked her bare left hand under her right.

Observing her action, Mike regained his confidence. 'You don't really expect me to believe it?' he asked, shaking his head. 'I mean, *you*, married...?'

His incredulity stung. 'Why not *me* married?' she demanded dangerously.

'Well, you're just not the type, Nat.'

Something inside Natalie snapped. 'Not the type to what? Need a hug occasionally, need someone to laugh at my jokes...need sex...?'

'*Natalie!*' Mike exclaimed in a shocked tone.

She gritted her teeth and planted her hands on her hips. 'Sex, sex, sex!' she parroted defiantly. 'Just because you don't fancy me, doesn't mean other men mightn't!'

'Well, you haven't had a boyfriend for the past five years—I'd say that speaks for itself.'

Natalie's shoulders slumped in defeat as the fight drained out of her. Of course he didn't believe it, who would? Sheer desperation had driven her to attempt a rash bluff and all she had done was make a total fool of herself. Rafe was never going to back her up—and why should he? If she was going to claim a fiancé it would have been wiser to chose a more plausible candidate.

'Well, she's got one now.'

The air rushed out of Natalie's lungs in one startled gasp. Her eyes flew to Rafe's dark, autocratic face. Even though she knew the possessive warmth in his eyes was for Mike's benefit, her responsive stomach muscles quivered.

'I don't believe it. You're just saying this to stop me getting Rosie,' Mike accused, sounding like a truculent child. 'It won't work.'

'Get Rosie?' Rafe frowned.

Natalie cleared her throat. 'Gabby and Mike want to take Rose to the States...' her face crumpled '...and I'll never see her again.' The disastrous wobble in her voice made her words barely intelligible but Rafe appeared to get the gist.

'Is that some sort of joke?'

Natalie blinked back the tears. '*He* says that they—'

'*He's* talking through his...' Rafe cast the other man a look that caused the shorter man to blanch and withdraw behind a chair '...armpit,' he finished acidly. 'And I suspect he knows it.' He lifted a strand of hair from Natalie's cheek and brushed away a tear with his thumb. 'He's trying it on, sweetheart,' he promised her.

'Now, you listen here...whoever you are...'

An ebony brow quirked. 'Natalie has told you who I am. I am the man she is going to marry.'

If it weren't for the possessive arm that snaked around her waist Natalie would have fallen in a heap. Instead she turned her face into the broad chest at her disposal. There was something very soothing about the steady thud of his heartbeat, as there was about the hand that came to rest on the back of her head.

'*You can't!*'

'I think you'll find I can.' While continuing to stroke the back of Natalie's head, Rafe lifted his eyes to meet the indignant face of the other man. His lips curled contemptuously. 'I appreciate that it must be hard for you to see the woman you lost with another man. I suppose,' he added thoughtfully, 'that it's at times like this we realise what we have lost—or in your case thrown away. There really is no mystery here. We've kept our relationship under wraps because it's a bit difficult as I'm Natalie's boss. We're off to visit my parents this weekend so if you don't mind we'd like to keep it quiet until then.'

Natalie admired his ability to improvise but she wished he'd keep things simple—Mike wasn't stupid.

'Then that makes you…?'

'Quite disgustingly rich,' Natalie supplied helpfully. She knew how Mike's mind worked. Despite his avowed contempt for money, he was always in awe of people who had it. A really horrid part of her was beginning to enjoy the sick expression on Mike's face.

'You've been sleeping with your boss?'

His tone of shocked disgust made Natalie flush.

'Well, actually, we haven't been getting a whole lot of sleep.' Rafe cupped her chin in his hand and tilted her flushed face up to him. 'Have we, angel?'

She was grateful that he'd decided to play along, but she wished he weren't doing so with quite this much relish. Already pretty messed up by the contact of his hard thigh against her own, her nervous system went haywire when he looked at her like that.

'I love it when you blush and, darling, happy Valentine's Day,' he told her in the manner of a man who found her totally fascinating and completely irresistible.

Natalie knew it was a lie but she was still mesmerised by the caressing light in his eyes.

Rose entered the room at that moment and her face lit up

when she identified the tall figure standing there. 'Rafe...Rafe!' she cried, bounding across the room towards him.

'Rose...Rose!' Rafe echoed, releasing Natalie.

Well, if nothing else had convinced Mike their daughter's rapturous greeting would have swung it. Natalie was concerned by the child's enthusiasm; now with Mike about to leave it was even more important that Rose didn't grow attached to a man who wouldn't be around for long. Natalie had no illusions—she didn't have anything that could keep a man like Rafe interested for long. It was something she'd have to deal with when the time came.

'Have you brought me a present?' the little girl demanded with innocent avarice.

'*Rose!*' Natalie cried in a scandalised tone.

Rafe didn't seem bothered. 'Next time,' he promised with a grin. 'Wow, cool shoes!'

'I look pretty.' Rose preened complacently.

'Beautiful,' Rafe agreed.

'You look beautiful, too,' she observed. 'Doesn't he, Mummy?'

A choking sound emerged from Natalie's throat. As hard as she tried to avoid looking at Rafe, like a compass needle finding north her eyes seemed irresistibly drawn to his.

'Men are handsome, Rose, ladies are beautiful.'

Rose shook her head. 'No,' she persisted stubbornly, 'Rafe is beautiful.'

Natalie could only agree with her daughter's assessment of the man whose startling blue gaze was melded with her own. Her voice thickened emotionally. 'Extremely beautiful,' she agreed huskily.

'Well, I think it's time that we were going,' Mike interrupted stiffly.

It was difficult to persuade Rose it was time to go, but eventually the time Natalie had been dreading arrived—she and Rafe were alone. There seemed no point delaying the inevitable; she took a deep breath and got straight to the point.

She shot a wary glance at the tall figure who was examining the books in her bookcase. He didn't *look*, but it was reasonable

to suppose, despite his performance, that he wasn't too happy
with her.

'I think Mike's in a bit of a huff.'

Rafe slid a copy of a paperback thriller back; he ran a finger
slowly down its spine before turning. There was a hard light in
his eyes. 'I don't think I'll be losing any sleep over your Mike.'

'He isn't my Mike,' she replied irritably.

Rafe's eyes narrowed as he looked searchingly at her. *'No…?'*

'He's getting married today.'

'Most people would consider him pretty good-looking,' Rafe
remarked casually.

'Fortunately Rose took after him in the looks department…'

'So you *do* think he's good-looking…?'

Natalie gave a bewildered frown. 'Look, just how are Mike's
looks important to anything?' she demanded.

'If he decided not to get married, if he asked you to take him
back—would you?'

Natalie coloured angrily. 'What do you take me for?'

His smile was cynical. 'A woman in love?'

Natalie's eyes slid from his. 'I am not in love with Mike,'
she replied guardedly. Now that she knew what being in love
actually felt like she knew she had never loved Mike in that
way.

Rafael gave one of his inimical shrugs. Natalie studied his
face. 'You didn't like him, did you?'

His jaw tightened. 'I didn't like the number he was trying to
do on you,' he revealed grimly. 'Give him custody? No lawyer,
no matter how well paid, could persuade a court in the country
to take Rose away from you.'

'You don't know all the facts.'

'I know you're a good mother.'

The conviction in his tone brought an emotional lump to her
throat. 'But I'm stony-broke. It's ironic, really Mike has never
been able to pay child support. Now he's marrying a rich
woman, his uncle has died and left him a property worth over
two million and the critics have decided he's the next Warhol!
I, on the other hand, expend more than I earn.'

'What I said still stands—you're a good mother and that's all any judge would be interested in.'

'You're sure?' Natalie said wistfully; she really wanted to believe him.

'Totally,' Rafe confirmed.

Normally Natalie found his immutable confidence irritating, but this was one occasion when she welcomed it. 'Did you go along with…?'

'Go along with…?'

Cheeks burning, she lifted her head. 'Me saying we were engaged. Was it because you didn't like Mike?'

'I expect that had something to do with it,' he confirmed.

'I suppose you expect me to apologise for…'

'Well, going on your track record I'm not expecting it any time soon.'

Natalie's head came up, she set her hands on her hips and glared up at him. '*I* don't have a problem apologising when I know I'm in the wrong—even to you!'

One dark brow lifted. 'Meaning I do?'

'You made me feel about so high,' she said, holding her forefinger and thumb a whisper away from one another. 'And,' she added bitterly, 'if you wanted to put me in my place you didn't have to do it in front of everyone! You didn't have to…' She broke off, dismayed to feel her eyes fill with tears. 'You probably don't even know when I'm talking about.' Why would he?

'I know.'

'I was stupid enough at the time to think that we were friends,' she added in a small voice.

'Yes, you were stupid,' he agreed. 'We could never be friends,' he added harshly.

To hear him spell it so brutally hurt more than she would have thought possible. 'What's wrong, Rafe—is my hair the wrong colour?' Rafe's eyes followed the movement of her fingers as they slid through the silky strands of her long brown hair. 'Or am I from the wrong social background?' she suggested scornfully.

'Your hair…' He cleared his throat and removed his gaze from her hair. 'Your hair is beautiful.' The forceful nature of this raw declaration made Natalie look at him sharply. 'And who our parents were has nothing to do with it.'

'Pooh…says you!' She sniffed.

His nostrils flared as she turned away from him. 'Yes, I do,' he rebutted in a driven undertone. 'And I say we couldn't be friends because there's too much chemistry between us and there has been from day one.'

Natalie spun back, her face flushed, her mouth slightly ajar. She could feel her fragile grip on reality slipping as she focused on his lean dark face. 'You're my b…boss.'

'I don't need reminding of that,' he promised her.

'Day one!' she breathed in a stunned undertone. 'You liked me…?'

'I don't think *like* is the correct term. Changing the subject slightly, which believe me I don't do out of choice…I was wondering…?'

'Yes…?'

'Are you going to the wedding like that?'

'Like…?' Frowning, she followed the direction of Rafe's gaze and gave a cry. 'Oh, God, what time is it?' she cried, drawing the gaping lapels of her thin, loose-fitting robe in her fist.

'Relax, it's early yet.'

'You wake up looking drop-dead gorgeous; for me it requires a little more time.'

'I think you look gorgeous like that.'

'If you're going to lie, try for something a little more believable.'

Rafe shook his head. 'My God, I've never met a woman as hard to be nice to as you.'

CHAPTER EIGHT

NATALIE smudged a little soft brown shadow on her eyelids and smeared some clear gloss on her lips. A quick flick of blusher completed her hastily applied make-up. It was ironic that the one time she had planned to really go to town with the warpaint she was in even more of a hurry than usual.

'Well, they do say the natural look is in this season,' she reflected, eyeing the result in the mirror as she fought her way into the simple soft apricot shift dress she'd decided to wear. It bore the label of a chain-store brand; Natalie had decided it would be foolish to try and compete on her budget.

She slipped her feet into a pair of high-heeled sandals that emphasised the shapely length of her slender calves and smoothed out a wrinkle in her fine lace-topped hold-ups she wore underneath. She glanced at her watch; it was the only jewellery, besides a pair of antique drop pearl earrings, she wore.

All I have to do now is something with this hair, she thought, frowning as she slid her fingers through the silky mass that fell river-straight almost to her waist. That was always supposing she *ever* got this darned zip up! She grunted softly and grimaced as she twisted around in an effort to see what the recalcitrant fastener had snagged on.

While in a position that would only be considered comfortable by a contortionist she lost her balance and stumbled against a lamp. She lunged for it, but her reflexes were not sharp enough to stop it falling off her bedside table, taking with it her alarm clock, which hit the metal bed frame and catapulted like a thing possessed across the room where it hit dead centre the cheval mirror, which shattered before her disbelieving eyes.

The noise as the glass showered onto the bare wood of the stripped floorboards was so loud that she wasn't aware of the door opening until Rafe was actually inside the room.

'I heard a noise.'

163

'I think they heard a noise half a mile away.' The wry smile that invited him to share the humorous side to this situation faded as her eyes encountered no reciprocal amusement in his—on the contrary Rafe's expression was unexpectedly severe, his entire manner off-puttingly grim as he stood there not reacting to the disorder around him.

Perhaps it was the thought of acting as her fiancé at the wedding that was making him look so bleak—now he'd had a little while to reflect he could be questioning if his acting ability was up to carrying it off.

Natalie was wondering if she ought to do the decent thing and give him the opportunity to back out gracefully when she caught sight of the neat stack of freshly laundered undies that were waiting to be put away on the bottom of her bed. Instinctively she reached across and drew the chenille throw that was folded across the bed over them. She realised immediately that all her prim action had done was draw his attention to them. He probably thought it hilarious that she imagined the sight of her white cotton knickers would inspire uncontrollable lust.

In your dreams! Maybe his too—*he* was the one who had mentioned chemistry. Lust at first sight, no less.

'Well, I suppose this means seven years' bad luck.'

'Are you superstitious?'

'Not especially—I have my fingers crossed.' So the joke had been pathetic, but a polite smile wouldn't have killed him! A frown deepened the line between her arched brows as she studied his enigmatic dark face. She was beginning to get the distinct impression that he hadn't heard a word she had said.

'My zip jammed,' she began to explain. When she was nervous she babbled and his silence and the growing tension she sensed in him made her *very* nervous. Also this whole bedroom thing was something she wasn't comfortable with. 'I guess it's a classic case of more haste, less speed. I was trying to unstick it and I knocked the lamp off.' She gestured to the lamp lying on the floor. 'It was sort of a chain reaction after that—you should have seen it.'

'Is it still stuck?'

His abrupt question made her start. 'What? Oh, yes, you have to be a contort—'

'Turn around,' he instructed brusquely.

'Oh, I'll manage.' She forced her lips into a smile.

'Turn around,' he repeated in a tone that suggested he was getting bored with the subject—and, for that matter, her.

Natalie bit her lip. If she persisted in resisting his perfectly unexceptional offer it might give rise to awkward questions, such as for instance why did the idea of him touching her skin have her in such a blind panic? After all, she planned on letting him do so as much as he liked.

'Thank you.' Taking a deep breath, she turned around to give him access to the zip.

Nothing happened; nothing happened for so long that she almost turned around.

Just as she was deciding enough was enough she felt cool air touch her skin as he lifted the mesh of her loose hair off her neck. A shiver slithered softly down her spine as she felt his fingertips lightly graze her skin. At that point Natalie realised this was going to be every bit as bad as she had imagined and more…*pure torture*!

Rafe eventually managed to gather all her hair in his fist. 'There's a lot of it,' he murmured, laying the heavy swathe over her shoulder. Displaying a meticulous attention to detail, he brushed the few stray strands that clung to her neck to join them.

'Did you say something?'

Natalie closed her eyes tight shut. 'Not a thing,' she assured him brightly.

There was another agonising pause before he reapplied himself to the task in hand. The zip was jammed just below her bra strap, and Rafe's fingers slid under the lacy hem to give himself better access to the problem.

'Stop fidgeting!' he snapped tersely as she shifted restively in a frantic effort to lessen the contact that was sending ripple after ripple of hot sensation through her body. Her skin was so hot and sticky he had to have noticed.

'Then hurry up,' she retorted thickly.

'I'm going as fast as I can.' He gave a grunt of pent-up frustration. 'Damned...stupid...!'

His touch had a frightening addictive quality. 'For pity's sake, it's not brain surgery!' she gasped, desperation in her voice. 'I have a wedding to get to.' And if she did or said what she actually wanted to she was pretty sure they wouldn't!

She heard him mutter darkly under his breath and felt his warm breath stir the fine hairs on her nape as he bent closer to his task. A faint whimper escaped from between her clenched teeth.

'You all right...?'

If she hadn't been so far from all right Natalie might have noticed that Rafe's normally assured voice held an unfamiliar strained note. 'Absolutely fine!' she heard herself lie breezily.

'I'm getting there.'

So am I—she was at that very moment hovering on the brink of a precipice; one little shove would have her turning around and begging him to take her. Exhaling gustily, she dabbed her tongue to the film of moisture above her upper lip. The debilitating weakness that was already severely affecting her limbs had obviously begun to cloud her mental judgement as well. Her suspicion was validated by the next uncensored idiot observation that spilled from her big mouth!

'Dear God, if you take this long to undress a woman the poor thing is probably asleep by the time you actually get started.'

'So far that hasn't happened; slow but thorough, that's me.'

The fiery blush travelled all over her skin, but underneath the embarrassment she was getting even more excited thinking about Rafe being thorough and slow with her.

Not now, there's a wedding to go to and all sorts of ground rules to figure out.

'Got it, I think...?' Holding the fabric taut, Rafe forced the zip upwards, it gave, and when he pulled it down again this time it slid smoothly—very smoothly all the way down.

All the way!

With a silken rush the peach-coloured fabric of the dress parted from her neck to the top of her tight buttocks and revealed the entire length of her satiny slim back, plus the interesting little dimple just above the soft curve of her peachy skinned bottom.

'Oh, *my God*!' The pressure inside Rafe's head was now so intense he knew something had to give. 'Oh, my God,' he repeated in a fainter but no less impressed tone. 'You're absolutely perfect.' He ran a fascinated finger down her straight spine, feeling the evenly spaced bony projections, letting his exploration widen to take in the elegant definition of her elegant shoulder blades.

With a mumbled imprecation that concerned his sanity, Rafe spun her around.

She stood there, visible tremors running through her slim body, eyes wide, lips parted. In the front the dress was hanging onto her slender shoulders—*barely*. One judicious tug and it would... Her wide eyes looked up at him; she was scared stiff he'd take the next step and scared stiff he wouldn't. Having suffered a similar ambivalence for weeks and months, he could readily identify with what she was feeling.

The dress fell with a sexy, silken slither to pool around her feet and Natalie stood there clad only in her minuscule lacy bra and matching pants; the stockings and high heels that completed the outfit she wore couldn't really be classed as clothing—more provocation!

Less is quite definitely more, Rafe decided, unable to stop staring like a kid at a sweet-shop window. No window...no door—in fact there was nothing keeping him away from her except his disintegrating will-power—an overrated virtue if ever there was one.

Natalie wanted to tell him that he really shouldn't have done that, but her vocal cords were paralysed—as she was—with lust. She waited for her protective reflexes to kick in, but they didn't. But then no man had ever looked at her the way Rafe was, and she felt her legs tremble.

'I've wanted you for weeks,' he confided, laying his hands heavily on her shoulders. 'I've fantasised about what you had on under those hideous, baggy clothes you wear.' He wasn't sure she was ready to hear what he had fantasised about doing once he had removed those clothes...fantasised about doing right there in his office.

Desire was like a fist clutching low in her belly. 'I dress for comfort.' She was surprised to hear an unfamiliar breathy voice emerge from her lips. 'Well, thank you for fixing my zip.' And blowing my mind into some lustful other dimension. 'But I really should be getting ready now.'

Rafe heard her out politely before he laughed scornfully and closed his hand possessively over her right breast. From the expression in his eyes it seemed to Natalie that he found the sight of her small breast covered by his big hand as stimulating as she did.

'I know a short cut to the church, we have at least forty minutes to spare.' He appeared to consider the problem. 'What do you suppose we do with that time?'

As he spoke he was scooping her straining breast out of the flimsy bra cup with practised ease. A sibilant hiss escaped through his clenched teeth as he watched the already engorged pink bud swell and harden. Natalie cried out and grabbed him by the front of his shirt.

'You are probably the smuggest, most conceited man that ever lived,' she accused shakily.

Rafe swallowed hard and dragged his reverent gaze to her face; there was not a trace of the smugness she accused him of in his raw, driven expression. Her stomach flipped.

He gave a strained, crooked grin. 'But sexy with it, *right*...?' he croaked hoarsely.

A laugh was wrenched from Natalie's dry throat—laughter and sex had never seemed compatible until now. 'It isn't your sex appeal that's in question here, it's my sanity—' She broke off mid-complaint as she felt the catch on her bra unclick.

With a smile Rafe chucked her bra over his shoulder. 'In the interests of symmetry,' he explained, admiring the perfect symmetry of her unfettered breasts. The thought of taking those straining peaks into his mouth aroused him unbearably.

Natalie could smell the warm male scent of his body. She wanted to touch him, wanted to so badly it blocked out every other thought. Feeling bold and reckless, she laid a hand flat against his chest; through his shirt she could feel the heavy thud of his heartbeat. His body was solid muscle and bone, a long, lean and lovely body. She gave a shudder of sheer heady anticipation and let her hand slide boldly to his flat belly. She felt the sharp contraction of his stomach muscles as he sucked in his breath.

'Sorry, I'm messing up your lovely clothes.'

She went to lift her hand but he caught it hard and held it there. His shimmering blue eyes scanned her flushed face. 'To hell with my lovely clothes!' he declared, releasing her, but only to tear the tie from around his neck. This followed the same path as her bra.

'There's glass everywhere—this is dangerous. You could cut yourself.'

No, you're the dangerous one, she thought, looking at his stern, predatory profile. Desire kicked hard in her molten belly, she shivered and her eyes darkened dramatically.

Without saying a word and correctly taking her compliance as written, Rafe swept her up in his arms, and picked his way through the shattered mirror towards the bed. Before he placed her down he removed the top cover, which was covered in tiny fragments of glass, and flung it to one side.

'Where are you going?' she asked plaintively when he didn't join her.

'I'll be right there,' he promised. His bright-burning eyes didn't leave her face for an instant as he stripped off his clothes with flattering urgency.

Natalie stared. She couldn't help herself—he was beautiful in a way that made her throat ache. His skin was an even dark gold dusted lightly in significant areas by erotic drifts of dark hair. The impressive strength of his upper body and magnificent, tightly muscled shoulders was perfectly balanced by a hard, washboard belly and long, long legs. Greyhound lean, he moved with the perfect co-ordination and fluid grace of a natural athlete.

He certainly had a turn for speed—in a matter of seconds he was standing there in just his boxers. As he stepped out of them Natalie caught her breath. She looked away, feeling like a guilty schoolgirl caught peeking.

Rafe gave a wolfish grin of predatory satisfaction. 'Don't mind me, I like you looking,' he confided with shameless candour.

The bed springs creaked as he landed beside her. There was no trace of laughter in his face as their eyes locked. Without saying anything he fixed his mouth to hers; it fitted perfectly. He continued to kiss her, deep, drugged kisses that sent her spiralling out of control and kept her there.

Natalie clutched at him, revelling in the smoothness of his skin and the hardness of his muscle. She didn't connect the soft guttural sounds that she could hear with herself.

Hands cupping her buttocks, Rafe drew her body into his. 'You can feel how much I want you...?'

Her body reacted as much to the sound of his voice as the erotic pressure of his arousal against her soft belly. Giving a fractured little sigh, she opened her eyes and tried to focus on his face...the outline was blurry.

'Are you crying?' Concern roughened his voice.

Natalie blinked and shook her head. The combination of lust and love was something she had never been exposed to before; she had no defences against the heady cocktail. 'I want you, too,' she whispered, touching him because she quite simply had to—*not* touching his silken length was no more an option than not breathing!

He groaned greedily and pulsed against the confines of her trembling hand. His uninhibited pleasure encouraged her to continue her erotic explorations.

It was Rafe who eventually stopped her teasing caresses.

'My turn, I think,' he announced throatily as he flipped her over onto her back.

Still ahead every step of the way, still anticipating what she wanted before she knew it herself, he slid down her body, caressing her with his hands, tasting her with his lips.

Her swollen, tingling breasts felt as if they were on fire after he had applied his clever tongue and hands to each quivering, pink-tipped mound in turn. She closed her eyes as he licked his way lower and when he reached the hot, drenched, sensitised region between her pale thighs her back arched, lifting her hips clear of the mattress.

Natalie hooked her fingers in his hair.

Rafe lifted his head. There were dark bands of colour high across his cheekbones. He took one look at her face and groaned. 'When you look at me like that I just want to...'

'So do I,' she moaned. 'So do, Rafe. Do it right now, you beautiful man!' she cried brokenly.

He kissed her neck as he settled over her. 'Oh, my God!' she moaned as he slid up into her, hard and hot. 'Oh, this is...is...' he rocked higher into her and she bit into the damp skin of his neck sobbing softly '...good...very, very good.'

'It will be...' he promised, thrusting hard. 'Just let go, let it happen,' he instructed, continuing to build a smooth, fluid rhythm.

Natalie didn't know what he was talking about, but she did know that she wouldn't mind if he carried on doing what he was for ever. A little while later she found out this wasn't true—in fact she couldn't bear it any longer. Just about that moment she discovered, in the most earth-shattering way, what he had meant—*it* happened!

In the aftermath of a climax that had involved her entire body from her toes to—well, she couldn't discount the possibility her hair follicles had been involved—she lay there in a dazed glow, curled up like a sleepy, sexy kitten in his arms. The only sound was her occasional murmur of, *'Wow!'* which made Rafe, who had his chin propped on top of her head, grin.

'I think I'm going to fall asleep,' she confided.

'Nice idea, but we might miss the wedding photos.'

With a horrified cry Natalie leapt out of bed, ignoring his warning cry of, 'Watch the glass!'

'Oh, God, we'll be late. Why didn't you remind me?' she remonstrated severely as she struggled into her clothes.

'I had other things on my mind.'

They weren't late and Natalie got to cry a little, seeing Rose looking sweet walking up the aisle behind the bride.

There was a certain novelty value attached to being the centre of attention. It aggravated the bride, too, which was a definite plus, but Natalie knew it wasn't her stunning good looks or sparkling personality that were the draw. No, it was the man beside her. That Rafe would inevitably know and be known by people on this sort of celebrity guest-list had not even crossed her mind.

She had reached the point, after two glasses of champagne, where she was actually enjoying herself when Mike introduced her as Rafe's fiancée. He did so in front of half a dozen people Rafe knew, one of whom, an opera singer of international fame, turned out to be one of his mother's best friends.

'Oh, Luisa didn't tell me and I only spoke to her on Thursday!' she exclaimed, kissing first Rafe and then Natalie on both cheeks.

'Actually, Sophia, we haven't told the families yet so I'd be grateful if you could keep it to yourself for a couple of days,' Rafe requested smoothly.

'But of course,' she promised immediately. 'And do your family know yet, Natalie?'

Natalie got the impression those bright, curious eyes were missing not a detail of her outfit.

'There's only my grandmother.'

'Oh, how sad, but you have a little girl, I believe…? A ready-made family—how nice for you, Rafe…but you have such a big family. Have you been to the *palazzo* in Venice yet?'

Natalie shook her head. *Palazzo!* That figured—blue blood on both sides.

'We'd planned to spend our honeymoon there,' Rafe slotted in smoothly.

'Oh, you will love it. Come along and tell me all about yourself, my dear,' she urged, drawing a reluctant Natalie away.

'I have never been so glad for Valentine's Day to end.' Natalie sighed later as she kicked off her shoes in the comfort of the car. Rose was already fast asleep in the back. 'I am so sorry!'

'About what?'

'About the fiancée stuff in front of your mum's friend. What'll you say to them?' she asked worriedly.

Rafe dismissed them with a shrug. 'Oh, I'll deal with them, don't worry.'

'You're being awful nice about this…?'

'I'm a nice guy,' he revealed modestly. 'Once you get to know me.'

Natalie lowered her eyes to her hands, which lay primly in her lap. 'I was wondering…' Was she making a terrible mistake?

'You were wondering what?' he prompted.

'I was wondering if you'd like to stay the night with me…if you've no plans, that is…'

There was a charged silence.

'If I had any I'd change them,' he told her with a grin that revealed his even white teeth. 'You have absolutely no idea how happy I am to hear you say that.'

'Well, I'm pretty happy to hear you say yes,' she admitted. 'The only problem is…I mean, I know that it's inevitable this thing between us has a relatively short shelf-life…'

'Is that so?'

His weird tone made her glance across at him sharply, but his profile was unrevealing.

'Well, of course,' she confirmed, determined to show him she didn't have any unrealistic expectations. 'I'm afraid…' she cast a worried glance at the child asleep in the back seat '…that Rose will get too fond of you. Perhaps you should keep your distance,' she suggested doubtfully.

'And how do you propose I do that?' he grated, not looking amused by her suggestion.

'I see what you mean. It's a pity you get on so well…'

'I can see how it might be more convenient if your child and boyfriend hated the sight of one another,' he drawled. 'For the record, I don't think it's a helpful thing to decide a relationship is doomed to failure before it's even started.'

Natalie blinked. Surely he wasn't suggesting they could have something long term!

He took his eyes briefly from the road. 'Why not see how things develop?' he suggested in a more moderate tone.

'That's fine by me,' she replied, trying to keep the jubilation and hope from her voice.

CHAPTER NINE

THE following Friday a week later Natalie was outside Rafe's office. They had arranged at breakfast to have lunch together. They had *done* lunch together twice already that week, and breakfast every day! A smile appeared in her eyes as her thoughts dwelt on an unshaved Rafe sitting at her kitchen table with tousled dark hair falling in his eyes... Sometimes she had to pinch herself, it seemed so unreal. But there was nothing imaginary about the growing selection of male toiletries crammed on the shelves in her dinky bathroom or the pair of black men's socks that had turned her white delicate wash a dirty grey.

The changes weren't restricted to her flat. Natalie felt a different person from the one she had a mere week earlier: happier, more carefree—simply more alive!

She had her moments of doubt. It wasn't just that Rafe had quickly become part of her life—he had become part of Rose's, too.

'Things are moving a bit fast,' she suggested tentatively to Rafe after the sock incident.

His deep blue eyes lifted from the journal he was reading. 'Do you mind?'

Natalie thought about it. 'No, actually, I don't,' she revealed with a silly grin.

Rafe responded with a grin of his own—one that was not at all silly. His grin made her heart race and her knees turn to cotton wool. He didn't raise any objections when she took the magazine from his hands and climbed onto his lap—none at all!

When she had asked Rafe what she ought to tell people at work, he had shrugged in the way only a Latin male could and said, 'Whatever you like,'—which was no help at all. On reflection Natalie had decided not to volunteer anything, but if

174

anyone asked she would tell them the truth, though sometimes she wasn't sure what that was, or where they were going.

She was totally, deeply, deliriously in love with Rafe, but how did he feel? Though expressive in many ways, shockingly so on occasions, he never once said 'love'. He told her how beautiful and sexy she was, but never once did he say he loved her. His restraint on the subject made her shy of expressing her own feelings, even though sometimes she *ached* to do so.

She was about to knock when she saw the door was ajar. She had pushed it open a little when she heard Rafe's voice inside; as she paused he switched seamlessly from Italian to English.

'Hold on, Mother, I'll put you on the speaker.'

His mother! Natalie, who had been about to move away, couldn't resist the opportunity of listening a little longer.

'Rafael, you don't call, you are never at home when I call and I've been so concerned ever since Sophia contacted me.'

The husky voice the other end was attractively accented.

'I asked her not to, so I was fairly sure she would. Why are you concerned, Mother?' Natalie could hear the sound of Rafe moving about the office—a drawer opening, paper rustling. She really ought to go—if he found her standing there eavesdropping it might be a little embarrassing.

'Do not be so obtuse, Rafael! Why do you think I am concerned? I know you were a little annoyed with your father...'

'*Annoyed!*' Natalie heard the sound of Rafe's harsh laugh. 'Why should I be annoyed? My father thinks he can arrange a marriage to suitable breeding stock, he puts me in an impossibly embarrassing situation...what is there to be annoyed about?'

'You know your father, he means well, but he—'

'Is a snobbish, manipulative, unprincipled... Do you suppose he's *ever* going to learn he can't run my life?'

'I know you're angry, I know you want to punish him, but really this isn't the way to do it!'

'What are you talking about, Mother?'

'I'm not stupid, Rafael,' came the impatient maternal reply. 'Remember what you said when I asked you about marriage— you told me then what the girl you married would be like. From what Sophia tells me this girl is the exact opposite.'

There was a short pause, during which Natalie held her breath; any desire to leave had vanished. 'You know, I haven't actually thought about it, but I suppose she is.'

'Add that to the fact this girl you so suddenly get engaged to just happens to be everything your father would dislike— divorced…with a child…from a totally different social background to your own… Am I supposed to think this is a coincidence? I know you want to teach your father a lesson, Rafael, but you have involved another person,' the husky voice remonstrated worriedly. 'Have you thought how this young woman is going to feel when she realises you are using her? I am assuming you are going to call a halt to this thing before you get as far as a church…?'

Natalie could have told her how *this girl* would feel—how this girl *was* feeling: numb. There was a total absence of feeling; she felt dead inside.

She turned and began to walk away, slowly at first and then quicker until she was running full pelt, oblivious to the startled glances she attracted. It all made sense, of course. That was why Rafe hadn't been angry when she had claimed he was her fiancé. He had seen it as the perfect opportunity to teach his interfering father a lesson—and the sex had been good, too.

My God, he must have thought it was his lucky day! She felt used and grubby and very, *very* stupid. She dashed a hand across her face as the tears started in her eyes. The numbness was beginning to fade, leaving a knot of pain that was lodged like a fist behind her breastbone.

'And all the while I was dreaming my silly dreams like the besotted idiot I am!'

'Ms Warner…Natalie…?'

'Yes, Maggie,' Natalie replied as she continued to empty the contents of her drawers into a bag.

'I just wanted to say…I'm sorry if…'

God, is this Maggie trying to be friends because she thinks I'm the boss's girlfriend? Ironic under the circumstances. 'Honestly, Maggie, you don't have to bother.'

'Oh, but I do, I *want* to! I think I might have treated you unfairly,' she began awkwardly. 'No, I *know* I did.'

'It's not nec—' Natalie began tiredly.

'I need to say this,' came the taut response. 'You made me feel guilty.'

Natalie straightened up. *'Guilty...?'* she echoed with a frown.

The older woman nodded. 'I had a baby, you see. I wasn't married and I gave him away...'

The simple statement hid half a lifetime of pain. Natalie's eyes filled with tears as her tender heart ached with empathy for the pain etched on the other woman's face.

'Oh, I'm so sorry, I didn't know.'

'Nobody did,' Maggie told her thickly. 'I made a choice, I chose my career over my baby. You didn't and, seeing you doing both so well, it made me ashamed that I had never even tried. Every time I looked at you I...' She shook her head and when she continued her voice was thick with emotion. 'I'm sorry I gave you a hard time.'

Natalie shook her head. 'It doesn't matter,' she told the other woman wearily. Nothing mattered any more, but Maggie's poignant tale had reminded her of something she still had—her daughter—and for that reason if no other she had to carry on. It didn't matter how bleak her personal future seemed, the luxury of falling apart was not an option.

'What are you doing?' Maggie seemed to notice for the first time that Natalie was removing her belongings.

With her forearm Natalie brushed the entire contents from her desktop into an open bag. She fastened the bag and straightened up. 'I'm leaving.'

Staying after what had happened was clearly out of the question. The idea of seeing Rafe on a daily basis made her blood run cold. She would take Rose for a holiday to her grandmother's, and when she was there she could sort out her options, such as they were. Maybe she would stay in Yorkshire? It had a lot to recommend it, the biggest selling point being the number of miles that separated it from Rafe Ransome. It was cheaper to live in the country. Grimly determined to be positive even if her world was falling apart, she told herself the country air would be good for Rose.

'Leaving! But I thought that you and...' Maggie stopped, colouring under Natalie's wry gaze.

'I thought we were, too, but I was wrong.' Natalie clamped her trembling lips together and, brushing past the other woman with her head downbent, fled.

Natalie found herself back at the flat; scarily she had no memory of how she'd got there. Once inside she began to put her plan—such as it was—into action. It was unlikely that Rafe would follow her, but if she was wrong, however, she had no intention of being here when he arrived. She gritted her teeth and blinked back the hot tears that filled her eyes as she haphazardly piled some of Rose's clothes and toys into a suitcase. She would pick Rose up from the child-minder and go straight to the railway station—yes, that was the best thing to do.

She was struggling as she lugged the second overfull case into the living room, when she hit her shin a painful glancing blow on a low table. If anything the pain was a useful distraction from the other pain... Sniffing defiantly, she placed her burden by the front door and looked around, trying to focus her thoughts. Had she forgotten anything vital? Mentally she ticked off items on her list of necessities. Her gaze fell upon an open book. It lay where Rafe had left it after Rose had climbed off his knee the previous evening.

'Tomorrow,' he had promised when she had begged him to continue. 'You heard what Mummy said—it's bedtime for you, young lady.'

An overwhelming sense of loss washed over Natalie, followed by a violent wave of anger. Rafe could have argued he had never lied to her—never told her he loved her—and it would have been true. She was willing to take a proportion of the blame herself, blame for falling in love with him. As far as Rose was concerned *nothing* could excuse his behaviour. That little girl adored him and she was going to be desperately confused and hurt to have him vanish from her life.

For that Natalie would never forgive him!

The sound of the key turning in the lock was very loud in

the quiet room. Natalie mastered her panic and lifted her chin
as she turned to face the door.

Rafe stepped into the room. Tall, devastatingly handsome and
very, *very* angry. Anyone with normal co-ordination and reflexes
would have fallen in a graceful heap over the pile of cases that
lay there, but not Rafe. Without pausing, he sidestepped the
obstacle without removing his burning gaze off the slim, rigid
figure who stood in the middle of the room.

Lips compressed, nostrils flared, his powerful chest rising and
falling as if he'd been running, he scanned her pale, hostile face
with his brilliantly compelling gaze.

'Going somewhere, Natalie?'

Natalie gave a contemptuous little laugh. 'Anywhere you are
not.' Her antagonistic reply was rewarded by his sharp inhalation. 'How did you know I was gone? No, don't tell me—the
loyal Maggie. You really do seem to inspire selfless devotion in
women, Rafe, but consider yourself with one less devoted slave.'
She placed her splayed fingers flat on her heaving bosom just
in case he was in any doubt of whom she referred to. 'You can
leave the key on the table when you leave.' She spoilt her dig-
nified dismissal by adding childishly, 'I suppose you'll be relieved not to be slumming it any longer!'

Rafe shook his head impatiently. '*Slumming it?* What the hell
are you talking about?'

'I did wonder that you never invited me to your place, but it
all makes perfect sense now. How would you explain me to
your friends?' With curious objectivity she observed the effect
of her words on his composure as the nerve beside his mouth
jerked.

'How could I suggest you spend the night with me when you
kept telling me how you wanted to keep the disruption to Rose's
routine to a minimum? Dear God, woman, you acted as if I was
trying to move in when I left a toothbrush in the bathroom!'

His ability to come up with a plausible excuse and then turn
the tables so that *she* was the one at fault was staggering and
probably, she thought angrily, the secret of his success.

'Sure, you're Mr Considerate!'

'Stop this, Natalie,' he pleaded in a low, impassioned voice.

'Stop what?'

The calculated obtuseness of her comment drew a harsh Italian curse from him. Swearing fluently, he crossed the room. As he reached her side Natalie was extremely conscious of his sheer physical power, of his tall, tightly muscled frame—he was a man in the peak of physical condition. In the past awareness of this strength had excited her; even now her stomach lurched as he approached. Contemplating the thrill it had given her to surrender to that strength increased her sense of self-loathing. With provocative deliberation she turned her head and looked away.

'What's going on here, Nat?' Rafe took her chin in his hand and tilted her head up to him. 'This morning things were fine, lunchtime you clean out your desk and walk out without a word...now I find you about to leave. Were you planning to give me any sort of explanation?' The screaming tension on his taut features brought his cheekbones into sharp prominence.

'No.'

Her monosyllabic response had much the same effect on him as a red rag did to a bull. 'Good God!' he thundered. 'You are—' He bit off the words he was about say and inhaled, breathing deeply as if he didn't trust himself to respond. When he did speak his low tone was flat and expressionless. 'Do you not think that I deserve to know what the hell I'm supposed to have done?'

Natalie gave an enraged yelp and tore her face from his grasp. 'You deserve—you deserve!' she yelled, her voice rising to a shrill, accusing shriek. 'You deserve to rot in hell, Rafael Ransome!'

He recoiled as if she'd physically struck him. If she hadn't known better she'd have bought that look of bewildered confusion on his dark face—if, that was, she hadn't heard that incriminating conversation and if she hadn't subsequently had her heart ripped out.

'I know, Rafe. I know.' She waited for him to at least acknowledge he had been caught out, but he didn't even have the decency to do that! 'So you can imagine why I find it a bit laughable you acting like the injured party here. I'm an adult, I should have known better,' she acknowledged, 'but I'll never forgive you for Rose. It was cruel, Rafe—you made her love you!' She pressed a hand over her mouth as a sob escaped.

'And I love her.'

Natalie gasped wrathfully. 'Why, you callous bas—!'

Rafe caught her hand mid-swing and brought it firmly down to her side. 'Now you will tell me what I am supposed to have done.'

Breathing hard as if she had been running Natalie raised her bitter eyes to his. They shimmered with unshed tears. 'There's no need to pretend, Rafe. *I know.*'

As if he could compel her to speak by sheer force of will, his piercing blue eyes narrowed on her face. '*You know…?* I'm glad one of us does, because I haven't the faintest idea what you're talking about. You know what exactly? Speak to me, Natalie, because you're killing me here.'

For a moment she hesitated; surely nobody could fake the raw emotional intensity and anguish she heard echoed in his voice. Then she remembered that damning conversation she had overheard and her face hardened.

'I know that you had your own reasons for pretending we were an item.'

Natalie hadn't known that she was secretly harbouring a crazy hope that this would all prove to be some horrible mistake until she felt it die. It died when he couldn't meet her eyes.

'And you think you know what those are?' he hedged.

'I know why you weren't bothered if your parents got to know about our fake engagement—you wanted them to.'

He shook his head, his brows drawing together in a puzzled line. 'Wanted them to what?'

Natalie gave an exasperated sigh. 'I heard you on the phone with your mother.'

A flicker of comprehension appeared in his strained eyes. As she watched his head fell back and he exhaled noisily. Bizarrely his attitude seemed one almost of relief.

'I took the call on the speaker phone…' He ran a hand across his jaw.

Natalie knew that by this time of day he would be able to

feel a faint stubble. Only yesterday she had complained about it
when he'd kissed her in the office lift and he had laughed. Actually she enjoyed the abrasive roughness against her soft skin.
The flood of heat that washed through her body was mingled
with anger and shame.

'Don't bother trying to remember what you said,' she advised
dully. 'I heard enough to make me realise I've been a total fool
to fall in love with you.'

Rafe's head jerked up sharply; his iridescent blue eyes
scanned her face. Whatever he saw there made the blood drain
from his face, his normally healthily golden-toned skin looking
greyish.

'*You fell in love...?*'

Clearly this was news to him and not welcome news. Maybe
he had a conscience after all? Well, that was good, because if
she felt this wretched it only seemed fair that he should feel a
little bit bad, too.

'So sorry if you didn't bargain for that, but don't worry, I've
woken up, I won't be proclaiming my feelings from any high
buildings.' The way I've been acting, I probably don't need to.
'I know that this has all been about you wanting to teach your
father a lesson. Everything falls in your lap, doesn't it, Rafe?'
she reflected bitterly. 'You needed an unsuitable sort of girlfriend and who comes along but the definitive version—*me*? The
sort of girl your father would cross the street to avoid being
contaminated by!'

'So *that's* it. You think...!' He shook his head and drew an
unsteady hand through his dark hair. Then unforgivably he
laughed—he actually *laughed*. This fresh proof of his heartless
callousness made Natalie feel physically sick. 'You were eavesdropping! Actually, Natalie, my father has been known to cross
the street to get a closer look at a beautiful girl but never the
other way around.'

'That only works if the girl is beautiful and I'm not.'

Her statement brought a stern, disapproving frown to his wide
brow. 'If I say you're beautiful, you are,' Rafe pronounced with
breathtaking arrogance.

'I have to be beautiful because you deigned to sleep with me, is that how it works? And don't expect me to apologise about eavesdropping—if I hadn't been I'd still be walking around thinking I was living out some sort of romantic fantasy.'

His eyes dropped to the lush curves of her full lips and then lower to the firm, uptilted outline of her small, pert breasts. He swallowed hard.

Seeing the contraction of muscles in his strong brown throat was the key that unlocked the door to forbidden memories. Memories of other muscles in his lean, firm body contracting and quivering beneath the glistening surface of his sweat-soaked skin and all in response to her touch.

She had almost succeeded in locking away the steamy memory when his heavy, darkly fringed eyelids, lifted revealing an expression so hot it could have started a forest fire. Natalie's pupils dilated until they almost obliterated the iris; similarly, the hormonal rush in her blood had a dramatic effect on her ability to think rationally—as in she couldn't! Sweat broke out over her entire body as she tried to drag herself clear of the sensual vortex that was sucking her deeper with each passing second.

'All my fantasies have you in,' he told her simply.

Goose-bumps broke out over her body as she suffered yet another dramatic shift in temperature. *If you believe this it'll hurt, Nat...don't believe...don't....!* She didn't allow herself to respond until she had regained some sort of control over her emotions.

'What is it with you?' she grated, trying to frame a reply that would make him realise he no longer had anything to gain from this pretence. '*I know*, Rafe, you don't have to keep up the act.'

'The only thing I've ever pretended with you, Natalie, is that I could control the way you made—*make* me feel,' he gritted with a self-derisive grimace. 'If you'd stayed around to hear the rest of my conversation with my mother you'd have heard me say as much to her. I left her in no doubt that she'd read things wrong.'

His hard jaw clenched as his brooding glance paused hungrily on the outline of her soft, quivering lips.

'The reason I didn't object when you introduced me as your lover was I liked the way it sounded.' Natalie's fractured gasp was clearly audible in the short pause that followed his words. 'As for playing your future husband, I had this idea that if I played the part really well you might decide to keep me on permanently.'

The blood drained from Natalie's face. *'Permanently?'* she parroted weakly. 'As in living together!'

'No.'

God, Natalie, will you never learn? 'Right,' she said, fighting for composure.

'As in married,' he slotted in coolly.

Natalie looked at her hands. They were shaking; so was the rest of her. This was all happening too fast for her to take in. 'But you said...'

'No, Natalie, my *mother* said. Think about it,' he suggested. She did.

An arrested expression crossed Natalie's face. *Rafe* had never actually said...had he...? Could she have jumped to the wrong conclusion?

'My mother is legendary for reading situations wrong.' His brows lifted. 'Now that I think about it, you two should have a lot in common,' he mused drily. 'Of course, if she had actually met you she would never have made that mistake. One look at you and she'd have seen that I'd be the luckiest man alive if you'd have me. Will you have me, Natalie?'

Natalie's heart was trying to batter its way out of her chest; the tight feeling her racing pulse created made it hard to breathe, let alone speak.

'What are you saying exactly, Rafe?' This time she wasn't going to jump to any premature conclusions.

A spasm of raw frustration flickered across his handsome drawn face. 'Do I need to spell it out?' he asked thickly.

'Well, yes, actually, I think you do.'

'Marry me, Natalie.' As her silence grew so did the tension in him. 'I think we make a pretty good team...'

Natalie widened her eyes innocently. 'So this is by way of being a business merger?' she queried pertly.

Their eyes touched; when Rafe saw what shone in hers the tension seemed to drain from his body. A fierce grin spread slowly across his dark face. 'Like hell it is!' he growled, reaching for her. 'Come here, you stupid woman.'

Resistance didn't even cross Natalie's mind as she walked into his open arms—where she belonged. His muscular arms tightened around her as his mouth found hers. The masterful kiss was raw, hard and hungry. Natalie's lips parted eagerly beneath the pressure. When they finally broke apart she was dizzy and insanely happy.

'Don't you ever, *ever* do that to me again! Do you hear me? I've aged about twenty years in the last hour.'

Natalie touched the raven hair at his temple. Despite his claim there was no sign of premature greying. 'Well, I wouldn't have jumped to the wrong conclusion if you'd told me how you felt,' she chastised him reproachfully.

One dark brow lifted. 'Like you did...?'

'I was afraid if I said anything I'd scare you off,' she admitted. 'And I felt that every time I tried to get closer you pulled back.'

'I was trying to be what you wanted—a low-maintenance girlfriend who didn't make demands...' She intercepted his wry look and grinned. 'Except in the bedroom,' she admitted guiltily.

'Let's leave the bedroom out of this for a few minutes,' he pleaded throatily.

'That's a first for you!'

Her saucy jibe earned her a long, lingering kiss.

When his head finally lifted Natalie gave a languid sigh and ran her fingers down the hard curve of his cheek. Rafe's eyes darkened as he caught her fingers and brought them to his lips. Quite deliberately he kissed each individual fingertip—Natalie found it incredibly erotic. He pressed an open-mouthed kiss to her palm before returning her hand to her.

'Is this real?' The air left her lungs as his arms tightened about her ribcage before dropping to the small of her back. The firm pressure brought her up onto her tiptoes and sealed their bodies at hip level so that she could feel—as he intended her to—the very real state of his arousal. 'You've convinced me,' she admitted with a husky chuckle.

'You see why I wanted to keep the bedroom out of this. I

need to say stuff and I can't think above the waist when you're like this.'

Secretly delighted at the image of herself as some sort of irresistible Jezebel, Natalie gave a sexy little sinuous wriggle that drew a deep groan from Rafe. She gave a regretful sigh and drew back.

'You're right, we should talk. How about if I sit over there—' she pointed at the sofa against the wall the opposite side of the room '—and you sit here.'

Rafe caught her arm. 'Too far.'

'And this is too close?' she asked huskily.

'It wouldn't matter to the way I feel if a thousand miles separated us,' he declared in a deep, throbbing accent. 'Oh, my love!' His blue eyes glittered down into hers as he laid his big hands on her shoulders. 'I think I loved you right from the beginning. When I told myself I was protecting you by keeping my distance, in reality I think it was more about protecting myself—I just wasn't ready to admit what I felt for you.'

'Are you ready now?' she whispered, hearing the thud of her own heartbeat in her ears.

She watched a slow, incredible smile spread across his face. 'Ready, able and very, *very* willing.'

'Oh, Rafe, I love you so much!'

The warm, sensuous impression left by his lips made her own tingle even after he had lifted his head. While she was smiling a little stupidly up at him he slid his hands down her arms until their fingertips were touching.

'I think this is about as far as I feel safe letting you go away from me...' he confessed.

'I'm not going to run away again, but...'

Rafe groaned. 'No more *buts*, please!'

'I love you but I don't want to be responsible for some sort of family rift. Your mother said your father would hate me,' she added worriedly.

He took her face between his hands needily. 'My father is many things, but stupid is not one of them.' The uncomplicated love revealed in his expression made Natalie's eyes fill with tears of sheer joy. 'It'll take him about two seconds to see you're exactly what he's been telling me I need for years. Within half an hour he'll have convinced himself it was all his idea.'

Natalie laughed. His certainty went a long way to easing her concerns.

'Forget my father, forget everyone, this is about us. We're a package deal: you, me and Rose,' Rafe declared proudly. 'Is that all right by you?'

'I think I might get used to the idea.' She laughed, throwing her arms around his neck. 'Given forty years or so.'

And Natalie was looking forward to every second of those years beside the man she loved.

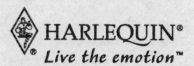

The world's bestselling romance series.

HARLEQUIN®
Presents

Seduction and Passion Guaranteed!

INTERNATIONAL
DOCTORS

They're guaranteed to raise your pulse!

**Meet the most eligible medical men of the world,
in a new series of stories, by popular authors,
that will make your heart race!**

**Whether they're saving lives or dealing with desire,
our doctors have got bedside manners that
send temperatures soaring....**

Coming in Harlequin Presents in 2003:

THE DOCTOR'S SECRET CHILD by Catherine Spencer
#2311, on sale March

THE PASSION TREATMENT by Kim Lawrence
#2330, on sale June

THE DOCTOR'S RUNAWAY BRIDE by Sarah Morgan
#2366, on sale December

**Pick up a Harlequin Presents® novel and you will enter a world
of spine-tingling passion and provocative, tantalizing romance!**

Available wherever Harlequin books are sold.

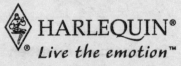
HARLEQUIN®
Live the emotion™

Visit us at www.eHarlequin.com

The world's bestselling romance series.

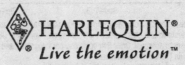